Visible

Book Four in the Ripple Series

Cidney Swanson

ISBN 978-1-939543-18-9

For Katie

Chapter One

GWYNITUDE

"Why is there a vehicle disguised as a UPS truck driving up to our castle?" I ask. My eyes narrow with distrust as a driver dressed in brown jumps out and deposits a large parcel one floor below my lookout. I pull back from the window so he can't see me. Or shoot at me. Or whatever he's planning.

"It's just a UPS truck," says Sam, sitting at the far end of the great hall. "They have them in France, too."

"Says you," I mutter. I am not a naturally suspicious person. A week ago, I would have mocked my future self for side-eyeing a UPS truck. But then, a week ago, I had zero personal experience in the care and drugging of hostages, or in being rescued by invisible ninja-friends, or in the proper disposal of bad guy bodies.

In the drive below, the man in brown dashes back to his truck and pulls around the semi-circular drive and down the avenue lined with tall dark trees. "It could be a bomb," I muse. "That would explain why he's in such a hurry to leave."

"Gwyn," says Sam. My best friend uses her "really?" voice.

"What? It could totally be a bad guy."

"It could totally be a driver with a long day ahead of him."

I cross my arms. "Whatevs."

"Sir Walter said he was ordering space heaters for our rooms," says Sam.

I rub my hands along my arms. Our current abode, Château Feu-Froid, lives up to the "*froid*" part of its name, for sure. Cold rock walls. Cold flagstone floors. It's freezing everywhere except in front of the fire. I walk the length of the hall, back to where Sam sits on one of two ginormous couches flanking a fireplace you could drive cars into.

"Space heaters, huh?" I ask.

Sam nods, idly running her fingers through her boyfriend Will's hair while he sleeps at her side.

Across the room, my mom is pacing, talking on her cell with my aunties. Again. Her sisters, who own several bakeries in LA, flew up to run ours in Las Abuelitas while we're stuck in France. From what I can hear of Ma's conversation, it sounds like they're making a mess of things at the Las Abuelitas Bakery Café.

I sigh and sink back into the feather-stuffed cushions.

"I need to get my Gwynitude back," I say. "Gwyns in their natural state are not paranoid. They are confident, independent, and fond of naps in warm corners."

"Not to mention, self-satisfied," says Sam.

"Exactly."

"So, like your cat Rufus," says Sam.

I glower. This, I am mortified to note, is also quite feline.

"Of course," continues Sam, "it is also true that Gwyns in their natural state have a boy hanging off each arm, which would tend to invalidate the 'independent' as well as the 'self-satisfied.'"

"I will not dignify that remark with a response," I say. She's hit a nerve though: I am very dissatisfied with my current boyfriend-less state. Fortunately, I have Big Plans.

Sam gives my hand a quick squeeze. "I'm just kidding," she says. "And I am all for the return of your ... what did you call it?"

"Gwynitude."

"That," she says. She drops her eyes, bites her lower lip. "I don't know what I would have done if anything had happened to you."

"Thank goodness for invisible ninja power, am I right?" I smile and the balance in our friendship tips back toward normalcy. Sam's job is to worry; mine is to be optimistic.

"You did amazing on your own, even without the ability to turn invisible," says Sam.

"Yeah," I reply. "My super power is the ability to annoy bad guys so much that they get sloppy."

"It worked," says Sam, shrugging.

It did, actually. I wasn't, shall we say, the most cooperative hostage when it came to making a proof-of-life video. That's what made the bad guys sloppy. And sloppy is what got my supah-friends and their supah-pals to rescue me.

I was drugged and asleep for the actual rescue, but that was fine with me. It gave them a chance to tidy up the bodies before I woke up. Woke up next to The Big Sizzle himself, Chrétien de Rochefort. Who was covered in blood, but that's another story. Cover him in blood, mud, or maple syrup, that boy, aka my Big Plan, is still smokin' hot.

I was supposed to have said goodbye to him the day before yesterday. And I did, too. No chance I was missing out on a proper French *au revoir*: two kisses on each cheek before I departed the country and Chrétien left on a mission with Dr. Pfeffer. But then the *gouvernement français* decided I shouldn't be allowed to depart the country without a passport. Hello. Bad guy didn't exactly give me time to grab my passport prior to the assault and kidnapping.

I am, however, remarkably cool with being stuck in France. (Occasional bouts of paranoia aside.) Yesterday, Chrétien came back from his mission with Dr. Pfeffer, and Pfeffer took Will's sister Mickie on

4

the new mission, leaving Future Boyfriend Material behind. Oh, darn.

Sadly, I slept in too late today to accompany future boyfriend into town this morning on a coffee and croissant run. As a consequence, my stomach is growling. I leave it to your imagination to determine with what kind of hunger.

"I'm starving," I say to Sam. She's preoccupied staring at her true love while he sleeps. Kill me now. "Did we seriously eat up all the bad guy leftovers?" I ask.

Ma, still on the phone, points an index finger at me and hisses like a tea kettle. She hates any mention of the dead bad guys. It's a Chinese thing. I think. It could be a Ma thing.

Sam glares at me, ordering me with her eyeballs to apologize.

I sigh and comply. "Sorry, Ma."

Ma says a few things in Chinese to her sisters, relative to the duty a daughter owes her mother, and crosses to the far side of the room.

It's not like I don't try. In fact, I've been the perfect, loving, respectful daughter for forty-eight hours. No wonder I want to goad my mother. It's like when you give a little boy a stick. Eventually, he's going to poke something.

Sam frowns. "I wonder how long 'til the people at Geneses figure out Helmann and the others are dead. Sir Walter said Helmann had very rigid habits checking in on his underlings, especially the ones in San

Francisco."

"You think someone will come and kick us out?" I ask. This is worrisome.

"They'd do worse than that if they knew the truth," Sam says. "At least, Fritz might, if he figures things out."

"Fritz?"

"Another of Helmann's sons," replies Sam. "Hans's brother."

"I thought they were all dead," I say. I totally did. A shiver runs along my arms.

Sam shakes her head.

"Oh," I say softly. "Fritz was the one who … operated on you. To steal an egg."

Sam nods.

"Do you think Fritz knows about this place?" I ask.

"Oh, he knows," says Sam. "Sir Walter has been keeping an ear out listening for Fritz's … what does he call it? Fritz's 'thought signature.' Which would indicate he's in the vicinity."

I sit up straighter. "Okay, why exactly are we staying here if Fritz might show up at any moment?"

"Convenience, mostly," says Sam. She looks down at Will. "Sir Walter wanted to give Will a couple days to mend. And then your thing with the passport came up."

"Hmmph," I grunt.

"I'm sure everything will be fine," she says. "And we can talk to Sir Walter about moving once he gets back," she adds.

Well, if my worrywart friend is cool with things, I guess I can try to relax, too.

"So, when's Christian—er, sorry, *Chrétien*, getting back?" I ask Sam, in my most disinterested voice. We called him Christian back in California, but then I found out he never really liked that name. And I will call him whatever it takes to coax that mouth of his into a smile.

"Same as the last time you asked," replies Sam.

"Oh, did I ask already?"

Admit nothing is my motto.

"Do your homework," says my mom, her phone call finished.

"How are the aunties?" I ask.

"They're running Las ABC into the ground. We have got to find a way to get home," she says, shaking her head. Then her eyes narrow. "Don't change the subject. Do your homework."

I've done my homework. It's not like I had anything else to do. Will found online copies of my textbooks and everything, and Chrétien wasn't here yesterday to distract me.

Ma adds, "You're going to need those straight A's with truancy on your permanent record."

"Ma." I groan her name so it's three syllables long. "There's no way they make truancy a part of my permanent record once the school hears why I'm stuck in France."

I say it like I'm sure, but my fingers creep up to

my mouth, *the little betrayers.* When I'm nervous, I chew my nails. Right now, I'm worried Sir Walter will say we can't tell the school why I skipped the country, which *will* result in my being marked truant.

"Stop chewing your nails," says my mom. "It's a filthy habit."

"Not if you keep your hands clean," I mutter.

Sam elbows me. I don't apologize this time. Me and my mom getting along isn't normal. And trust me when I say I could use an extra large serving of normal after the events of the last week.

At least I'm still in one piece, though. Beside Sam on the couch, Will has a broken leg in a walking cast. Christian—oops—*Chrétien* and Dr. Pfeffer took gunshot wounds. I guess Will has it the worst though, judging by the amount of pain relievers he's taking. He sleeps, like, most of the day, so Sam is getting about as much action in the kissing department as I am.

I have got to stop thinking about kissing. I wonder what Chrétien is thinking about right now. Probably, how he wishes he was still out there helping Mickie and Dr. Pfeffer. With Sir Walter's guidance, Pfeffer is going to buildings owned by über bad guy Girard Helmann and searching for hidden invisible people. Who are hypnotized to stay asleep until a password wakes them up and brings them visible. I am not making this up. I couldn't make this up if you paid me.

And it only gets better.

Helmann (the chief of my abductors) wanted to

use the sleeper agents to "vaccinate" people. He told the sleepers they would be saving lives. But really, they were intended to inoculate non-members of the so-called Aryan race with a very, very deadly virus. Fortunately, my super-friends put the kibosh on the planned murder of billions of innocent people by these sleepers.

So now, all the sleepers can either be left forever invisible and insubstantial (and asleep, obviously), or someone can wake them up and "re-educate" them. Pfeffer voted for saving them, and Chrétien tried to help. But apparently, Chrétien's mannerisms and his odd way of saying things make the sleeping army people wary. Mickie and Pfeffer say that, in the early stages of sleeper re-education, trust is critical. Hence, Chrétien's hasty retreat back to my side. With which I am totally cool.

"I don't think they'll mark you truant," Sam says, bringing me back to the present. She is still fussing with Will's hair. She does this, like, all the time. Like he's a cat in need of grooming. For the record, I would never do that to Chrétien.

Sam continues. "The French government refused to let you leave the country. It's not your fault. Anyway, my dad can talk to the school board if it becomes an issue."

"We don't need special treatment," says my mom. Her mouth pulls into this narrow line with which I am unfortunately familiar.

"Ma," I groan. "We do. We totally do."

My mom looks about to say something, but instead she folds her arms across her chest and mutters under her breath in Chinese. That's the thing with Bridget Li. Anytime she's unhappy, it's all Chinese.

"Did I ask to get kidnapped?" I demand. "It's not my fault I can't get back to school."

Sam shifts uncomfortably on her couch. She thinks it's her fault Helmann's son Hans kidnapped me—to lure her out of hiding.

"And it was totally nobody's fault in present company, either," I say, bumping shoulders with my best friend.

There's a prolonged silence before Sam gives me approximately forty percent of a smile. I have got to watch what comes flying out of my mouth. One of these days, one of my flip remarks will take someone's eye out. I slouch lower. I wish Chrétien would come back with those croissants already. I stare at the door, willing it to open.

And then, because apparently I can make things happen with the power of my mind, the heavy oaken doors into the great hall creak, announcing an arrival. Look who has super powers *now*.

We have oak doors on the Las Abuelitas Bakery Café, but these doors? They are *OAKEN*. Like something from *Lord of the Rings* that makes you want to roll your R's with a Scottish accent. Or whatever. It's been a few boyfriends since I watched LOTR.

Sadly, my mind powers aren't functioning

optimally. I appear to have conjured Sir Walter instead of Chrétien. I mean, nothing against Sir Walter. He fathered Chrétien, after all. For which he has my eternal gratitudinousness.

"Good news, my friends," says Sir Walter de Rochefort as he crosses the room to meet us by the fire. The great hall, in spite of essentially being the Chamber of Death and Blood, is where we tend to hang out, even though Ma doesn't like it. (Her thing with dead people.) But we hang out here because it is freaking February at the 48th parallel, and that means it is colder than a witch's kitty, and this is the one room with central heating. By which I mean the fireplace of obscene proportion.

Sir Walter stokes the bonfire and tells us his good news. "The local constabulary has agreed that you are not a felon, my dear *Mademoiselle* Gwyneth, and has agreed to ask no further questions as to your appearance within France."

Dude. That must have cost a lot. I keep the thought to myself because Ma is uncomfortable owing someone for as much as a sugar cube. She has no idea everything Sir Walter's done for us.

"In addition," continues Sir Walter, "he has returned to me your dear mother's passport." From inside his pocket, Sir Walter produces the passport of one Bridget Li, naturalized citizen of the US of A. "And as soon as we can arrange for your own passport, *Mademoiselle* Gwyn, to be sent here, the local agents have assured me we will have their complete cooperation in returning both of you to the *Etats-Unis*."

Sir Walter originally offered to take us back home invisibly, but Ma flat-out refused. Apparently her one experience rippling with Sam and Chrétien through the central California foothills was enough to last a lifetime.

Ma tries to look happy, but she is totally not happy with the prospect of spending more time inside our current residence. I can tell by the way she jams her hands under her legs, so she won't be tempted to chew her own nails. The acorn doesn't fall too far from the tree there, let me tell you.

"I don't suppose you have something … *official* that I can forward to my school?" I ask.

Sam raises an eyebrow a few millimeters.

Okay, let's just say I haven't *always* been this concerned about school grades and truancy and so on. I mean, I get straight A's (*definitely* a Chinese thing), but I usually act like I don't care. And so would you if Ma was your mom and breathing down your neck about grades and honor and the future, like, twenty-four-seven.

I guess you could say something has changed for me. Being kidnapped, drugged, threatened at gunpoint, and waking to a room with blood everywhere probably qualifies for life-changing.

"However," continues Sir Walter, "the French idea of complete cooperation is, shall we say, somewhat different from what you have been accustomed to in your own *Etats-Unis.*"

Ma's hands, under her thighs, clench into tiny fists. She would rather eat her own fingers than chew her nails in front of people.

"There is no cause for concern," says Sir Walter. "However, you must prepare yourself for things to move at a French pace. That is, a *leisurely* pace. Fearing you might, *Madame* Li, become bored during your enforced confinement in *la France*, I have made certain purchases recommended by your daughter."

It takes me a minute to remember what these purchases were.

"Purchases?" asks Ma, looking suspicious.

Oh, right. *Those* purchases.

"I gave Sir Walter the ingredient list for your famous chocolate chip cookies. He's never had any," I say. "Isn't that the saddest thing ever?"

The corners of my mom's mouth turn slightly upward with pride. Her cookies alone could keep the Las Abuelitas Bakery Café in the black. They are that amazing. Back in Las Abs, Ma makes twelve dozen assorted cookies a day. Every day. It was actually Sam's suggestion that we get Ma baking again. *It will help her feel normal*, Sam said. *Like Sylvia with her garden.* Only, it turns out bad guy kitchens don't come stocked with chocolate chips and brown sugar. It would probably upset the balance of the universe if they did.

For what it's worth, I think Sam's a little wrong about baking making Ma happy. I've seen Sam's step-mother Sylvia weeding her garden. It makes Sylvia

13

happy. Ma baking just makes her a less anxious Ma.

But in any case, my mom takes the bait, rising and following Sir Walter to the kitchen. As she goes, I hear her complaining about how Sir Walter shouldn't have spent his own money and how she is totally going to reimburse him.

"Seriously?" I say. "Why can't she just tell him thank you?"

Sam shrugs, neutral. She's a natural diplomat. Unlike *moi*.

"I'm sure your mom doesn't mean to be rude," said Sam. "She's just been through a lot."

"She *is* rude, whether she means to be or not. She's just like her older sisters. Heaven forbid my aunties should ever owe anyone for anything."

"So I guess this means you're stuck here in France with me for a few more days," says Sam, tactfully changing the subject.

It works. She's introduced a subject that makes me smile.

"I prefer to think of myself as stuck in France with Hunkalicious from the seventeenth century for a few days."

And then it occurs to me Sam might be intending to hang out with him, what with Will knocked out on pain killers. Sam and Chrétien are long lost cousins, after all. "You're not planning on spending every hour commandeering Chrétien's time, are you?"

"Me? No. Will's still a little ... *sensitive* about me and Chrétien. Which is ridiculous."

14

Will stirs but he doesn't wake up.

"Ridiculous," I agree, nodding like a bobble-head toy.

Sam laughs. "It is. Chrétien is like … he's like the brother I always wanted."

"Not remotely attractive to you."

"Afraid not," said Sam.

"*Not* is good." Not makes me smile again. A self-satisfied cat smile. "*Not* is excellent. So let's plan operation Gwyn Catches Chrétien."

Sam laughs. "Let's not."

I give her puppy eyes, for which she is a total pushover. Will *always* has puppy eyes, which is fine, I guess, if you like that kind of thing. Myself, I prefer manly *I am a knight from the seventeenth century* eyes.

"Come on, Sam. I need your help here. How do I get Chrétien to notice all this?" I run my hands over my chest and down to my hips. "Okay, so maybe there's not a lot to notice up top, but I could get a push-up bra. You think they sell those in France? They have to, right? The French probably invented the push-up bra."

"If you believe the new Victoria's Secret ads," says Sam, shrugging.

"Great! Let's go bra shopping," I say, standing up. "Actually, I could use an overhaul in the panty department too. And these jeans? The button's loose and, ugh! They do nothing for my assets." I slap my hands on my backside.

Sam shakes her head sadly. "Chrétien would

15

rather die than let his eyes rest on your, um, assets. Of any size or location."

I exhaled heavily. "You are no help at all." She's also dead wrong. I've seen Chrétien examining my assets. It makes my insides go all soft like melting ice cream.

"I hope my passport gets lost in the mail," I say. "A few weeks with Chrétien sounds heavenly. Even in the Castle *de* Kidnap."

The sound of Chrétien's voice from inside the kitchen catches our attention. He must have come in by the service door.

"Croissants!" says Sam. "Yummy!"

"Chrétien!" I say. "Yummier."

Sam's eyes fly to the ceiling. "You're hopeless."

"*Au contraire*, my friend. I am full to the brim with hope when it comes to your hot-tastic cousin. Speaking of which, why are we in the Chamber of Guns and Needles when Chrétien is in the kitchen?"

Sam's eyebrows pull together. "You need to stop referring to this room as 'the Chamber of Needles' and stuff like that around your mom, okay? She's freaked out enough as it is."

"I know. That's why I'm doing it around you."

Sam rolls her eyes.

"Cut me some slack, girlfriend," I say. "I'm the one stuck here with a parent."

I tug my shirt down, give the girls a bit of a lift, and generally prepare to make an entrance into the kitchen.

"Are your folks enjoying their second honeymoon or whatever?" I ask as Sam tries to get up without waking Will.

Sam nods. "It's actually their *first* honeymoon. They didn't want to leave me alone when they got married."

Sam's lucky. Her dad and step-mom are more or less cool with her missing school to stay behind while Will recovers. Of course, bad guys burned her house down, so she doesn't really have a home to return to at the moment.

From the kitchen, I hear Chrétien's laughter, throaty and *very* sexy.

"Come on. Let's go grab those tasty buns," I say, waggling my eyebrows.

Sam shakes her head. "Really?" is all she says to me.

For the record, I may be guilty of exaggerating my intentions for the sake of shocking my best friend. It's just so much fun. Like what I said about little boys and sticks.

We don't actually make it to the kitchen, though. Sir Walter strides toward us, saying, "Sit, sit. My son brings the croissants in a moment. Coffee, as well."

He coaxes the fire back to a four-foot blaze. Smoke from a fire that hot would bring the Las Abs Volunteer Firefighters to your door *stat*. And, speaking of *le hot*, here comes Chrétien, bearing a tray with croissants and coffee.

Fresh from an hour outside, his face is all

17

strawberries and cream. Someone: *give me a spoon.* Maybe it's a seventeenth century thing to have that alabaster skin, those bright red cheeks. I remember thinking some of the portraits in the Louvre exaggerated the pale skin and red cheeks, but maybe that's just what everyone looked like. In which case, give me a spoon *and* a time machine.

Ma accepts a croissant while telling me to do my homework. She waves her phone at me. "Your teachers forwarded another assignment."

"Oh, goodie," I say, checking out someone's derrière as he leans over to pour coffee. My. Just … *My.*

Sam elbows me. She's so protective of Chrétien. Honestly, what does she think I'm going to do to him?

I hold out my hand for Ma's cell and glance through the email. "I did this assignment early. Sorry, Ma. Afraid I'm still caught up. Except for that French paper *Madame* Evans assigned a month ago. Ugh."

"It wasn't that bad," says Sam. She's already done hers.

"I hate that assignment," I reply. Then I have an idea. "Do you think *Madame* would accept a report on 'What I Did During My Enforced Stay in France' instead of the history paper?"

"No," says Sam. "And it's not like you've been getting out and trying to speak French, either."

"I offered to go undergarment shopping, but *someone* wasn't interested," I say. I glance at Chrétien, but he must not know the English word "undergarments." Or he's too polite to acknowledge my use of the word.

"Anyway," I continue, "why should we have to re-write history? It's a stupid assignment. History's already been written. By definition."

On the other side of Sam, Will shifts. Opens his eyes.

"It's an easy paper," says Sam.

"Did someone say 'history'?" he asks.

I smile and shake my head at Will. "Do you have any idea how much of a cliché you are?" I ask him.

Sir Walter hands him a croissant. Will grins. I don't know if it's for my remark or for the breakfast.

"Anyway," I say, "there's nothing easy about this paper. There is no way I finish it on time."

"Yeah, if you don't start, it's kind of hard to finish," says Sam.

I stare at her. Sarcasm is like this new hairstyle Sam's trying on lately. I'm not entirely sure it looks good on her. "You are a cruel friend, Samantha Ruiz."

Sam just sits there looking smug.

I guess she's right about the paper. It's not an awful project, like the annotated bibliography for American Literature or the AP Biology project we worked on with Will earlier in the year.

No, the French class paper is simple, comparatively speaking: find something interesting about a French king or queen and turn it into a four page paper. Sam wrote hers on Marie Antoinette and what parts of the Sofia Coppola film were accurate.

She consulted Sir Walter, so she didn't have to visit a bunch of moldy internet history sites.

I look over at Chrétien. He's done with his croissant, and now he's licking his personal fork and knife clean. Apparently, in his day, this was good manners. You carried your own knife and fork in a box everywhere you went. The habit bugged me at first, but I have to confess, there is something about watching him tongue that flatware clean that shivers my timbers.

And just like that I'm struck with a brilliant idea. I could totally interview Chrétien about whoever was king in the bring-your-own-flatware era. There are probably a million things I could ask Chrétien about. Sixteen hours a day's worth, easy, for the next week or two while I'm stuck in France. I feel very warm inside in a way that has nothing to do with the hot coffee in my hands.

I shoot Sam a text.

What historical era is Chrétien from? I'm going to ask him to help me with my paper.

She looks down at her phone and reads what I wrote. Then she looks back up to me, mouthing the word *pathetic* to me. She texts me a non-response.

I've told you Chrétien's not looking for a relationship right now.

I respond right back.

And who says I am? Maybe I just want a way inside his—

Beside Sam, Will leans in to read over her

shoulder, and I see Sam hastily deleting my message. She also tucks her phone in her jeans, ending the conversation.

"What was that you were saying about your homework?" Ma asks me, brushing croissant crumbs from her lap.

"Gwyn was just texting me about getting started," says Sam.

"Gwyn was most certainly not," I retort.

Sam smiles and shakes her head.

"Gwyn had best remember who provides her with food and shelter and get busy," says Ma.

"Anyway," I say, ignoring Ma, "I still need to pick a king. A good one. A hot one who had lots of hot royal assignations."

This makes Chrétien's face flush, and he rises, gathering empty croissant plates and napkins.

Ma speaks in rapid, angry-sounding Chinese.

"Just kidding, Ma," I say, sighing. Then I rise and give her a hug. I really shouldn't provoke her right now. She's been through a lot.

But then, so have I.

"How about the prince who married Cinderella?" I ask.

It's my peace offering to Ma. My mom and I have a *Cinderella*-palooza every Valentine's Day where we watch all the different movie versions of the Cinderella story. We eat chocolate and hug and cry a lot and it's sort of when we hit the "reset" button on our relationship for the year. We missed out this year,

21

obviously, because: *kidnapped*. But, by mentioning Cinderella, I'm reminding her I still love her.

"What have you got for me, Will? The story's French, right? *La Cendrillon?*"

"The story of Cinderella is make-believe," says Will.

"It must have been based on *something* historical, though," I say.

Beside me, Sam murmurs, "Drop it." Her face is serious. She really means it.

I give her a look that says, *The heck, Sam?*

Ask me another time, she texts me, her eyes fixed on Chrétien.

My eyes narrow. Chrétien takes the plates and the tray to the kitchen.

"If you want a good paper topic," says Will to me, "you should pick Louis Quatorze, *le Roi-Soleil*. The Sun King. He and Chrétien were born in the same year," he adds.

"Tell me more about *le Roi-Soleil*," I ask Will, just as Chrétien comes back to the great hall.

Chrétien is preoccupied, leafing through an old book with a worn leather cover.

"Well," says Will, "The Sun King ruled seventy-two years although technically his mother was regent for the first—hey—" Will interrupts himself and opens his computer. "There was some big breaking news about his mother the day before yesterday. Some scandal about her maybe abducting or poisoning her son Louis's lovers…." He breaks off and searches for whatever he found the other day.

"Yuck!" I say. "I'm not doing a paper on abductions. Too close to home, much?"

"It was really interesting," Will says.

"No," I reply.

"Okay. Well, if you want to start with the basics on the Sun King himself, this is a good site," he says, passing me his computer.

"I'll go work over there," I say, indicating the massive table running the length of the room. I wonder how I can get Chrétien to come join me.

Sam rolls her eyes at me. I swear she reads minds.

As I stand, I flip my black hair dramatically behind my shoulders. Chrétien looks up from his book. He loves my hair. He said so. He called it the color of ravens' wings.

"Time for homework in the *Chambre de la Morte*," I say as I cross to the table.

Sam shakes her head at me.

I hold my hands out in a silent gesture of "*What?*" It's not like Ma knows what I said is French for *Chamber of Death*.

But as I stand to go to the big table and study, Karma pays me back for being a disrespectful daughter. The formerly loose button on my jeans pops clean off and goes skidding across the stone floor, coming to rest under the chair Ma is sitting in.

"Great," I mutter, grabbing at the waist of my jeans so they don't fall down. I must have lost some weight during the day and a half when The Hans and

Franz Show didn't feed me anything but snooze-inducing drugs. I walk over to retrieve the button.

"Ma, do you mind?" I point under the chair. "My button?" I can't get under the chair unless she gets up.

"If you please," says Chrétien. He sets his book down and totally dashes to my side. *Dashes.* "Be so kind as to allow me to retrieve what has been lost."

Oh, you can retrieve anything you want with that accent and that dashing.

"Not necessary," murmurs Ma, shoving the chair back a few feet.

But Chrétien bends over and retrieves the errant button, holding it out like a prize he's just won.

"If you will permit," he says, "I can sew the *bouton* for you." He's already reaching for his *cadena*, the little box where he keeps his personal knife and fork along with a needle and thread, wrapped in a thin piece of leather. Chrétien was training as a tailor when his dad came and claimed him and introduced him to life at the French court, and he said keeping the needle and thread helped him remember where he was from when he sat down to lunch with royalty.

I murmur something grateful to Chrétien. I am all for him sewing me back into my jeans. I mean, in theory, I'm all for him getting me out of them. But when he has his needle all ready, he stares at the button like it's something written in a foreign alphabet.

"This is no *bouton*," he says, finally.

Ma takes it from his hands and examines it. "It's a snap," she says. "You would need a rivet press

24

machine to fix this."

I groan. "Of course it couldn't be a simple button. Anyone have a belt I can borrow, because, hello, there's a little too little Gwyn to hold these jeans up."

"I didn't pack one," Sam says.

Ma shrugs. "Me neither."

Of course no one has a belt. But then I smile, a tiny gleam in my eyes. "That's it. I'm going shopping. Ma, I need euros. Sir Walter, I need car keys."

"You are not going shopping by yourself," says Ma, rising like she's coming along.

Now, I love my ma, but I have been on enough shopping trips with her to know she is the last person I want to go shopping with in France.

"Sam can go with me," I say. "Ma, you owe Sir Walter those chocolate chip cookies. After he bought all the ingredients."

Ma frowns. Like I said, she hates owing anyone anything, so I've totally got her. The frown becomes a glower, and she strides off to the kitchen. So I am down one interfering mom. Yay! But I'm also minus any cold hard cash. I consider re-engaging The Ma. However, my mom's stingy. It will be easier to get her to pay someone back a large amount than to get her to give me a large amount up front.

"Can I borrow a hundred euros?" I ask Sam.

She reaches for her money.

I ask Sir Walter again for car keys.

"Let's go," I say to Sam.

Only, Will has drifted off to sleep again, his head

in her lap. Disgustingly sweet. She looks at me with a face full of apologetic.

"Fine," I say. "I'll go alone."

Sir Walter clears his throat. "Perhaps," he says, "considering your mother's concern as well as … our general circumstances and your own, ah, less than complete command of the national language …" He looks pointedly from me to Chrétien.

Chrétien nods like he's agreeing with something.

I bristle. "My French is totally adequate." But then it occurs to me Sir Walter was implying Hunktastic should come along with me.

Oh.

Oh, yes, please.

"Of course," I add quickly, "it probably would help my mom to worry less if I had someone along who could help out in a pinch."

Chrétien bows. "It would be a great honor to accompany you upon your *visite* to the tailor of the local … how is it you say *village* in English?"

"Village," Sam and Sir Walter say together.

"Right," I say. "Let's go find us a tailor."

"Wait a sec," says Sam. She fiddles with something on her bag and then holds a safety pin out to me. "A quick fix. You're going to need both hands to drive."

She's right, actually. Chrétien doesn't drive. And Sir Walter's car has a clutch, which means I'll need both hands *and* both feet to drive.

"Good thing I know how to operate a stick," I

mutter as we take off.

"To my great shame, *Mademoiselle*," says Chrétien, "I understand not the operation of the horseless conveyance."

"I could totally teach you to drive, you know," I reply.

He does a little bow but doesn't say anything.

We reach the bottom of the marble staircase where I pause before the front door because the stupid safety pin doesn't want to go through all the layers of jeans, and I figure I should probably secure my jeans before venturing out of doors. "Give me a quick second," I say. I manage to stick myself in the thumb. "Ouch!"

"*Mademoiselle?*" asks Chrétien.

"It's this stupid safety pin. What a ridiculous name. There's nothing safe about a pointed metal stick." I suck my wounded thumb. Which I am sure looks so … mature. Exhaling heavily, I try again. And jab my thumb again. At which point I might have uttered a strong expletive.

"Allow me," says Chrétien, holding his hand out for the safety pin.

He gets down on one knee and takes both sides of my jeans in his long-fingered hands. The back of his knuckles brush beside my belly button. His hands are warm. His touch is electric. Like, actual electricity is pumping through his veins and it leaps across to me.

I have dated a lot of guys, but none with electricity instead of blood in their veins. Oh, boy. I am in deep.

I look down at Chrétien. The safety pin is giving him trouble, too, by the look of things.

"I beg pardon," he murmurs. "I have nearly finished."

The back of his hand brushes my belly again. More electricity.

"No worries," I manage to say in this breath-y voice for which I would totally mock Sam if she ever used it. In fact, I think I have mocked her for something like that back before she and Will were an item.

"There we are," he says, and he smoothes the waist of my jeans with both hands.

Oh. My. Gosh.

"*Voila*! Good as new," he declares.

In spite of all the things I say to Sam about Chrétien, what I'm feeling at the moment can only be described as … bashfulness? Shyness? The consequence of electric shock? I'm not sure what the correct label is. I do, however, know this feeling is not an ordinary component of Gwynitude. Judging by the flash of heat along my neck, my jaw, my face, I am turning bright red. I mutter a quick *thanks* and push on the door. Outside, in the February air, my blushing won't be as noticeable. I hope.

Chrétien makes this noise under his breath. It's very French. It takes me a second to place it as his disapproving noise. I pause, trying to figure out what he doesn't approve of.

Ah. The door. It probably caused him actual, physical pain to not hold the door open for me.

"Sorry," I say, looking at the door as he pulls it shut.

"We are in *la France* now, *Mademoiselle*. You must allow me to behave according to the local customs."

"Fine," I say. "You can open every door for me until we get back to the *château*." I don't even know if he's right about this being a local custom. It's been a few centuries since he lived in France. But I guess I can survive having Chrétien open doors for me for an hour.

"Okay," I say as we climb into Sir Walter's car, "we shop for jeans first. Then shoes. Then lingerie." I wonder for half a second if Chrétien knows that word. Then it hits me the word is French to begin with. Duh.

"Your state of preparation for a stay of this duration must have been poor," says Chrétien.

"Yeah," I say. Hans didn't exactly let me pack. "You'd think Ma might have grabbed me a spare pair of … um … *socks*." I was totally not going to say socks, by the way, but I chickened out actually saying "panties" out loud in front of Chrétien. Which will be interesting, seeing as I'm about to go panty shopping with him.

The universe has a strange sense of humor.

I shake my head as I shift into third gear. Then, just as we pull out from the *château*'s long drive, I notice a black car parked across the road. No one inside.

"Does that strike you as suspicious?" I ask Chrétien.

Chapter Two

EVERYONE WEARS JEANS

I downshift into second in order to pass the black car more slowly and get a good look at it. Expensive. Blacked-tinted windows in back. French license plates. Empty.

Suspicious.

But after giving the car a visual "once over," Chrétien doesn't appear concerned. In fact, he teases me. "*Mademoiselle* Samantha told me of your concerns regarding the delivery carriage."

"Delivery carriage?" I frown. "Oh. The UPS truck. Yeah." I sigh. "I guess I need to recover my chill."

"You have endured a great distress," says Chrétien, earnestly. "Only the passage of time will bring about the recovery of chill."

"Recovery of chill?" And now I'm the one laughing.

I drive Chrétien to the closest town without running over anyone or anything, and my French home-stay last Christmas taught me how to find parking in France, so pretty soon we are walking through the charming village of Vieilles Dames looking for someone who will sell me jeans.

"Are you quite certain," begins Chrétien, "that the females of France don the same manner of apparel as the females of your own land?"

"Everyone wears jeans, Chrétien. Everyone."

He does this little head-shrug that makes him look like Sir Walter. If Sir Walter was fifty years younger and hot enough to deep fry wonton strips. (Not a very authentic Chinese food, by the way.)

"Ah," he says, indicating a sign with an extended hand. Chrétien never points with his finger. "*Le Petit Tailleur.*"

I stand to one side of the front door, allowing him to hold it open.

Inside, Chrétien mutters to me that this doesn't look like any tailor-shop he's ever seen in France. What it looks like is total fantasticness with price tags in euros. It's the colors that hit me first. Oranges! Plums! Magentas! Back in Las Abuelitas, I can guarantee you everything in La Perla Fashions, our one clothing store, is spring green, spring pink, or ivory. Ma colors.

Here, everything is Gwyn colors. I squeal just a

little bit and dive into the first row of hangers I reach. The prices are a bit ... depressing. As in, I am on a trip for jeans, shoes, and panties. I do not have money for a plum scarf to top a burnt orange sweater over a magenta micro skirt.

Sighing, I hit the jeans rack, find the cheapest pair there and ask, in imperfect French, where I can try them on.

The saleswoman, in perfect English, directs me to the side of the store where I cram myself into the world's tiniest changing booth and somehow manage to undo the safety pin on my old jeans without drawing blood. The contenders for "Gwyn's new *hawt* French jeans" have a crazy high waist. No way does anyone west of New York City dress in jeans like this. But when the saleswoman has me come out to check the fit, I see Chrétien do this little double-take followed by his cheeks turning pink, so I figure I must look okay.

"I'll take them," I tell the saleswoman. "*S'il vous plaît.*" Fifty-five euros later, I have a pair of jeans.

"Shoes, next," I tell Chrétien.

"Your current footwear, I confess, has troubled me."

"Oh, yeah? You don't think flip flops are the way to go in the dead of winter?"

"The topless slippers are called 'fleep-flops'?"

I laugh at his accent. 'Cause it's either laugh or, you know, swoon. But before we find a purveyor of footwear, we pass a lingerie shop.

"Ooh-la-la," I say, passing a manikin wearing a bustier and the world's tiniest panties.

Chrétien just stares, his eyes giving away nothing of whatever he's thinking. But I'm guessing no one put stuff like this in window displays back in the day.

After nearly pushing the door open myself, I step to the side and allow Chrétien to hold it open for me.

"*Bonjour, Mademoiselle. Bonjour, Monsieur,*" says the shopkeeper.

"*Bonjour,*" I say back.

"Ah, *Américaine,*" says the shopkeeper.

"*Oui, Madame,*" I say back.

"And your *petit-ami,* he is also visiting from … another land?" She takes him in, head to toe, and doesn't peg him for American, apparently.

I would so love to say he's visiting from another time.

"Oh, he's not my *petit-ami,*" I say instead. Not my boyfriend. Tragically.

"Well, let's just see what we can do to change that," says the shopkeeper, conspiratorially. She pulls a measuring tape from where it drapes around her neck, pushes my arms out to the side and starts measuring my boobs.

"Oh, no, no, no," I say. "I just need some panties."

"Mmm," she intones in this completely French way which somehow conveys to you that you are wrong and that she knows better. She does this all with one letter of the alphabet. "Mmm."

I totally need to learn how to do that.

Chrétien, meanwhile, has drifted close enough that I feel his breath on my shoulder.

"May I?" he says, extending a hand toward the measuring tape.

Omigod, there is no way I'm letting him measure anything on me.

"With the numbers marked already?" he asks, examining the measuring tape. "But, how clever!"

"They don't have that when you came from?" I ask, surprised.

Chrétien shakes his head.

Neither of them notices my substitution of *when* for *where*.

Chrétien thanks the shopkeeper and returns the measuring tape, still gazing at it in utter fascination. Which, considering the variety of ... *undergarments* surrounding the two of us, takes some powers of concentration.

I sidle up to the clerk so I don't have to talk loudly.

"I'm a small," I say. "In American sizes. What do you have that's low-cut in front and won't go up my butt cheeks in back?"

The clerk hands me half a dozen panties from these teensy drawers along one wall of the shop and directs me to the changing area. "Let's see how we do with these, shall we?"

She turns to Chrétien. "You would like to accompany your little friend?"

I don't blush easily (ask Sam), but my face is heating up like a super nova. "I think he's good waiting out here," I say. Chrétien himself seems to have been rendered speechless by the question.

I so did not see this shopping expedition in a clear light when Chrétien offered to come along.

I hold up one pair of panties in front of the mirror, check the price tag, and decide I can afford half a panty if I still want to buy shoes.

"Great," I mutter.

"We are doing well, *Mademoiselle*?" asks the shopkeeper.

"Oh, yeah," I say. But I must have said it too quietly, because she's pulling back the curtain next thing I know.

"Hey!" I say. Kind of loudly. As in, loud enough to attract Chrétien's attention away from the bustier he was examining a second earlier.

He sees me, standing there with my jeans around my ankles, and I am just so grateful I didn't actually, you know, drop my drawers. Also, if I thought I couldn't blush any worse a minute ago, I stand corrected by my full body blush right now. I tug the curtain shut, hard.

"Sorry, sorry," says the shopkeeper. "*Elle est charmante*," she says to Chrétien.

I can't hear his answer. Thank goodness. I struggle back into my new jeans and grab two pair of panties that look least likely to bug me, and as I exit the fitting room, I keep my eyes anywhere—*anywhere*—

but on Chrétien.

Who seems to be in a conversation with the shop owner about one of the bustiers, of all things. I so do not want to know how that topic arose between them. I pay and we leave and my cheeks begin to return to a nice neutral Asian color.

"I was to have been trained in the construction of ladies' bodices," says Chrétien. "*Bustiers*, you see? The pay was as good as for gentlemen's coats, and my mother was ambitious for my future. I am told the bustier makes a surprisingly comfortable undergarment."

"Ah," I say. And for once in my life, I don't come up with a provocative reply. At this point, all I want to do is gather the scattered shreds of my self-respect.

Chrétien maybe picks up on this, because he changes the topic. "The *mètre à ruban*, the measuring ribbon, I believe? It was remarkable, was it not?"

"Measuring tape," I say. "Yup. Remarkable."

Maybe he wasn't changing the topic for my sake after all. I mean, seriously, of all the things Chrétien could have found remarkable just now: the measuring tape? Me-in-my-bikini-cuts didn't even make the list? The last time I felt this disappointed was when I found out the guy in the red suit wasn't the one putting toothbrushes and candy in my stocking.

"Let's go home," I say.

"We cannot return without your slippers," says Chrétien.

Shoes. I'd forgotten. I dig in my jeans pocket. I

have seventeen euro. Nope; there's another ten.

"I don't think I'll find much for twenty-seven euros," I say.

"You possess not the certainty of this."

Dear God, I love how he talks. His voice is what chocolate would be like if chocolate were a voice instead of a food group.

"Here we are," says Chrétien, opening another door.

I sigh heavily and walk inside.

"*Bonjour, Mademoiselle et Monsieur*," says the shoe salesman.

"*Bonjour*," we reply at the same time.

"*Américaine*." He chews the word like it tastes slightly off in his mouth.

"What do you have for twenty-seven euros?" I ask.

He sniffs, air rushing in through his nose, and the sound is so stereotypically snobby Frenchman that I almost giggle.

"*Je vais chercher*," he says. He will look.

He asks my size, which I have learned in European sizing is thirty-five, and I reply, "*Trente-cinq*." Which I so wish was my bust size instead, but that's a whole other issue.

"*Excusez-moi, Monsieur*," calls Chrétien, bristling with indignation. "*Vous n'avez pas mesurer sa taille*."

"It's fine," I say. "He doesn't need to measure me. I'm a thirty-five. I promise."

The clerk stops in his tracks and turns. He

glowers at Chrétien. Chrétien glowers back. For a minute, it looks like the two might punch each other, but then the salesman pulls out a foot measurer and plops it on the ground next to me. He takes my foot like it might bite him, and without so much as glancing at the numbers, he says, "*Ah, oui. Trente-cinq.*" He then breezes to the back of the store.

Chrétien mutters under his breath in French and the shoe salesman mutters under his breath in French, and I browse the *haute-couture* high heels section, wishing the universe had seen fit to gift me with the ability to walk in heels. There's a pair that are seriously blinged out. I'd like to see Ma's face if I came home with them. I reach out to hold one up: gold lamé, fake diamonds across the straps. They are gorgeous.

Monsieur returns a moment later. "Just as I feared. We 'ave not your size."

Chrétien takes the gold lame sandal I was drooling over a second ago and shoves it in the dude's face. "We will purchase these. Size thirty-five."

"Chrétien," I murmur. They cost three hundred twenty euros. "I don't have enough."

"I do," he says to me. To the clerk, he says, "A thirty-five. *Rapidemente.*" Quickly.

"*Non, non,*" says the man. "I regret we do not have that shoe in such a size." He turns to me with a very fake smile that stops short of his eyes. "We do not, as a rule, cater to your … type."

My type? The type with twenty-seven euros to spend?

Chrétien makes this noise in his throat that sounds like growling. "What do you mean, 'her type'?"

The salesman flicks his fingers in the air as he speaks. "Her ... *type*. Her *couleur*. Her ... *race*. Small feet and ... so on."

Chrétien strides to the salesman, pausing to grab a pair of gloves that are displayed on the counter. And he freaking *slaps* the salesman with the gloves. Seriously. Glove-slap.

"*Vous me donnerez satisfaction, Monsieur?*" says Chrétien.

Which I think means, will the dude sell Chrétien the shoes or not.

But I don't want them anymore. I don't want anything from this horrible person or his horrible store.

"Let's go," I say.

Chapter Three

RED SHOES

Inside the shoe store, Chrétien stands his ground, waiting for an answer.

I grab his hand and tug. "I want to leave. Now."

Chrétien says over his shoulder, "*J'habite Château Feu-Froid.*"

"Why did you just tell him where we live?" I ask, shaking my head. I don't want that creeper knowing where I live, even if I only live there a week.

"Should he decide to accept my challenge, he must know wherein I dwell, must he not?"

"Your ... challenge?"

"Yes. I struck him and offered to fight for your *honneur.* How do you say it?"

"Honor," I reply. "You seriously offered to fight a dude who was rude?"

41

"Of course. He insulted your good name and your national origin."

I can't help myself—I laugh. Like, full on giggle.

Chrétien raises one gorgeous eyebrow. "You are amused?"

"I'm honored. Truly." I giggle again. "But no one duels over racism in this century. Well, they might fight wars, I guess, but no dueling."

Chrétien looks puzzled. "That is most illogical. A duel is settled between two persons. A war involves thousands."

"Yeah," I say. "I guess it isn't logical. But that's how things are."

Chrétien does the nose-sniff thing like the snobby shoe clerk. The French have so many ways to communicate that don't involve words. *Madame* Evans should totally let me do a paper on that.

"Let's go home," I say.

We are halfway back to the parking lot when I notice an adorable slip-on shoe in a window display. In cherry red. I have such a thing for red shoes.

"Do you mind?" I ask Chrétien.

"Of course not," he says, executing a mini-bow.

We enter through the world's narrowest door, all carved in flowers and vegetables. Inside, the shop is a hodge-podge of shoes, bicycle tires, fishing rods, and things I can't identify by name in French *or* in English.

"*Excusez-moi*," I say to a white-haired lady in the back. "*Est-ce-que vous avez cette chaussure en trente-cinq?*" I point to the front window display, to the red shoe,

42

hoping I've just asked if she has it in my size.

"*Bonjour, Mademoiselle. Bonjour, Monsieur,*" she says, smiling from ear to ear. She is missing at least three teeth, but her eyes sparkle and she rushes to one side of the store where she pulls down a box marked "35" on it.

She opens the box, gesturing and speaking all at once. "*Asseyez-vous, Mademoiselle.* Sit, sit."

But there's only one shoe inside the box. Which just figures. I am doomed to never find shoes in the village of Vieilles Dames. The old woman has crouched down to open the box at my feet, and she wheezes like anything as she stands upright again.

"*Attendez,*" she says. "Wait, wait." And she hobbles to the front of the store. "*S'il vous plaît, Monsieur?* Please to help me, young man?"

Chrétien follows her and reaches down inside the window display to grab the shoe we saw from outside. He walks back to where I am seated. The old lady holds out her hand for the shoe, but Chrétien shakes his head, keeping the shoe from her.

"*Non, non, Madame,*" he says.

And then he does the sweetest thing. Having seen how hard it was for her, he won't let the old woman bend over again to put my shoe on. Instead, he gets down on his own knees and removes my flip flops himself. My heart does a funny little leap. He picks up the first shoe, the one from the box, and slips it gently over my toes. Grabbing the back of my heel, which I am so glad I loofahed last week, he pulls the rest of the shoe onto my foot. His hands are soft and warm and basically I am turning into a melted puddle of Gwyn-goo.

"How does that feel?" he asks.

And I know he means the shoe, but that is so not the question I am answering when I say, "Fantabulous. Totally."

He smiles, one side of his mouth pulling up higher than the other one, and reaches for the other shoe. Okay, I have always thought it was seriously weird to have a thing for feet, but I have to say, I could develop a thing for having Chrétien touch my feet.

"Do you like?" he asks.

"Perfect," I say. "Just perfect." I'm *so* not talking about the shoes.

"How much is the price?" he asks the white haired lady.

"Oh, *laissez-moi penser*; let me think. How about fifteen euros?" She grins her missing-teeth smile and I hand her a folded up wad that contains twenty euros.

Chrétien and I are on our way out when she comes hobbling after me. "You paid too much," she says, frowning. "*Attendez*—wait."

"It was a tip," I say, grinning. "For extraordinary service."

"Ah," she says. "*Un pourboire*. Well, I will drink to your good health *mes enfants*! *Au revoir!*"

"That was most kind of you," says Chrétien.

I shrug. "I think in the 'Battle of the Kind,' you

come out the winner."

He looks at me funny, employing one of his little head shakes. The sun catches in his eyes, making him squint. His eyes are hawkish, narrowing to the sides. I wriggle my toes in my new red shoes and feel this warmth creeping all the way up my legs and arms and settling in my heart. And then everything inside of me is just bursting, and I grab Chrétien's hand, and we run all the way to the car, breathing hard and smiling like idiots.

But by the time reach the drive to Château Feu-Froid, Chrétien's gone all quiet. He's a million miles away from here. The black car is still sitting by the side of the road, but he doesn't take the opportunity to poke fun at me about it.

I pull up the lonely drive and see Sir Walter striding back and forth before the castle, his head tilted like he's worried about something. Or listening for something.

Chapter Four

DUMBEST COMPLIMENT EVER

But by the time I set the parking brake, the worried look is gone. Sir Walter is all smiles. He opens my door.

"Everything okay?" I ask.

"Oh, yes, yes," he says. He strokes his goatee. "Just my idle imaginings, it would appear."

Turning to his son, he asks, "Your expedition—was it successful?"

"Indeed," says Chrétien, quietly. "If you will excuse me…."

He leaves the rest of the sentence just hanging there in the air and strides up the stairs leaving me alone with the Six Hundred Year Old Man.

"I got what I needed," I say. I can feel my cheeks turning pink as Chrétien marches back up the stairs to the great hall. Why's he so eager to run away? I thought we were having fun.

"I don't get him one bit," I mumble under my breath.

Sir Walter chuckles softly, which makes me realize I said what I was thinking without thinking about what I was saying. Not a new thing for me, sadly.

I meet Sir Walter's eyes, and they are full of compassion. For me? For Chrétien?

"He is searching to understand himself as well, I think," says Sir Walter.

Interesting, but hardly helpful.

The wind kicks up a pile of leaves and pine needles in the drive, pushing them against the stone façade of the *château*.

"You know," I say, "back home, all I have to do is snap my fingers and any guy I'm interested in comes running."

Sir Walter chuckles.

"It's true," I say. Possibly with a defensive edge to my tone. Because it *is* totally true.

"I doubt not the truth of your claim."

"But Chrétien doesn't seem to notice me at all." My eyes narrow. "Does he not like girls?"

"He has no inclinings toward his own gender, if that is what you ask."

I nod. "So is it just me he doesn't find attractive? 'Cause I'm ... you know ... not Caucasian?"

"*Au contraire, Mademoiselle*," says Sir Walter. "He has spoken of your beauty within my hearing."

"He has?" My heart races a bit faster. The wind tosses more leaves at the castle.

"He described you as *exotique*, I believe."

"Really? Exotic?"

Exotic's good.

"My son was born in an age given to the spontaneous praise of beauty. Beauty was seen as an accurate reflection of character. The more beautiful the exterior, the more perfect the soul."

"Oh," I say. "So, he thinks my soul is beautiful?"

Dumbest compliment *ever*.

"Ah, *Mademoiselle* Gwyn," says Sir Walter, sighing. "Will you walk with me?" He extends his arm, crooked at the elbow. Back home, my mom watches enough costume dramas that I know what to do. My arm slips into his. As we walk forward together, part of me chokes up a bit; I've never had a dad. I bet Sir Walter was a good dad.

"Perhaps *Mademoiselle* Samantha has told you some of my son's story?"

"I know he was married. I know he slept in the wall of your family castle for a few hundred years. I've been meaning to ask Sam about that, actually."

"He lost his wife. There was a child as well. Madeleine. She was the apple of his eye."

"Oh," I say. "That's so sad."

"She was his step-child, the daughter of another, but he loved her as his own. She died of the same illness that took his wife."

"That's awful," I say. And then I remember to

add, "I'm so sorry for your loss."

He gives my arm a little squeeze. "Time has healed my wounds. In fact, I begin to think I was wrong to suggest to Chrétien that he hide himself away through the centuries. Perhaps, had I not, he would be through the worst of his pain."

"Oh," I say. This certainly explains a few things. Chrétien's not looking for love. He's looking for pain relief. I look up at Sir Walter in time to see him swipe a tear from the corner of his eye.

"The wind, you know," he says. "It blows so fiercely."

I nod. He doesn't wish to be caught crying.

I get that.

"I'm sure you did what you thought was best at the time," is all I say.

"Yes, yes. A father is so powerless in such a situation. I would take his sorrow for my own if I could. But of what worth is my sympathy?"

"Hey!" I say, turning so I can look him squarely in the eye. "As a daughter with absolutely zero in the dad department, I'm here to tell you that your sympathy is worth the world. Do you know what I'd give to have a dad that cared a rat's ass about my existence?" I glare at him. "Pardon my French," I add, apologetic.

"Your ... French?"

"It means, pardon my swearing. I should have said 'a rat's backside' to be polite. At least, in the world according to Ma."

Sir Walter chuckles. "Your mother has more than

made up, I think, for the absence of a father in your life."

I raise one eyebrow at him. "Are you sure we're thinking of the same person?"

A smile is all I get for that. Half a second later, Sir Walter tilts his head to one side. "My son calls," he says.

He must have the world's quietest vibe on his phone. That or the wind drowned it out. Or his weird thing with hearing voices that Sam mentioned before.

"You will please excuse me," he says, with a little bow.

I watch him disappear around the corner of the *château*, trying to decide if I'm ready to face (1) Ma and (2) my French paper. Honestly, I'd rather wander the abandoned grounds. I need to think through what Sir Walter said about Chrétien. I mean, Sam's dropped hints about his heart being ... *unavailable* or something. But "unavailable" and "grieving my dead wife and child" are two really different things.

Suddenly, I feel embarrassed about how hard I've been trying to get his attention. Of course, maybe he didn't notice. Yeah. Sure. I groan and turn the corner of the building. How am I supposed to act around Chrétien now?

Possibly, I could stay outside all day and avoid him. There's less wind on this side of the castle. I kick at a pile of decaying leaves and twigs. A few spiders scurry away, terrified. That's me, stirring up trouble again. I should relinquish my title as Queen of

Relationships. In favor of something like Queen of Messing Up Relationships.

Sighing, I sit on a stone bench and look at my surroundings.

It's actually sort of beautiful: the wildness, the decay. This side yard must have been a garden hundreds of years ago. It's not tidy, like Sylvia's garden. It's not bare gravel, like my back yard with the cat kennels. It's ivy crawling over hidden lumpy things. And cedars swaying in the wind. Although, they could be firs or pines. I can't remember how to tell them apart. During fifth grade Outdoor School, I kept busy rating boy kisses on a scale of my own devising, crushing the souls of my prepubescent admirers.

"Ugh!" I cover my face with both hands. The history of How Gwyn Treats Boys does not, perhaps, reflect my better nature. I really need to turn over a new leaf. Right now, besides Chrétien, there are at least two other guys in my life. Well, Jake hasn't texted me for two days, so maybe he got the message regarding my low level of interest, but José is definitely still in pursuit. I may, possibly, have engaged in a little harmless flirting with José. And now he won't stop texting. My strategy so far has consisted of ignoring the every-other-hourly texts. Ignoring is a step up from leading him on, right? Somehow, I don't think Sam would agree.

I sit up straighter. That will be my new motto: *What would Sam do?*

From inside the pocket of my new jeans, my

phone vibes. Probably José. Perfect. Just the chance I was looking for to flip over that new leaf. I grab out my cell. But it's my mom, asking what happened to me and thoughtfully pointing out that my French paper is not going to write itself.

Coming, I type.

But I don't move.

Instead, my mind wanders back to Chrétien. Sir Walter worries he made things worse for his son by stuffing him in ripple limbo for over three hundred years. Is he right? Maybe Chrétien still has all his grieving in front of him. I'm a little vague on the whole "how time passes" thing with regard to rippling.

The chill from the stone bench has now numbed my backside. I stand and stretch.

It doesn't really matter, though, whether or not Chrétien has had enough time to recover. There's this whole ocean of different between us now that I know his story. An ocean made up of things like marriage and sex and parenting and death. Plus, he's Catholic and I'm not. He's serious and I'm ... Gwyn.

I can't think of a single thing we have in common.

Except for our devastatingly good looks. Obviously.

Nice. I'm totally alone and I'm trying to make jokes. I need a twelve step program for the terminally flippant.

I hear feet treading on the gravel just around the corner. Ma feet. Ma always walks like she's trying to sneak up on you.

52

A good daughter would go apologize for making her mother hunt her down like a lost cat. I am hardly a model daughter, and we've already established my shortcomings in other areas, but you've got to start somewhere, right?

I rise, an apology on my lips.

But it's not Ma.

It's not anyone I recognize.

Chapter Five

MISS CONGENIALITY

I slip out of the stranger's line of sight, hiding behind a large shrub. It's a man, talking softly on his cell. I can hear everything because he's walked right over to the bench. *My* bench. If it weren't for the wind, he'd probably hear me breathing. I try to breathe more quietly, just in case.

"You've heard nothing from my father, then? Or any of them?" asks the stranger.

I don't like his voice, and I have a bad feeling about his identity.

"Of course I'm solid," he says, irritated. "How else would I place a call?"

The wind scatters leaves as the stranger listens to the response. I can't hear the other caller.

The stranger grunts. He kicks at the detritus

underfoot. "It's just as likely Father decided I wasn't important enough to merit an update. There's smoke billowing out the chimney, though, so he can't be far. And an expensive Alfa Romeo out front. Flashy. Just the sort of thing Hans likes."

I gulp. Hans? That is a name I could go the rest of my life without hearing again. But with this man talking about Hans, it's a safe bet I'm spying on Fritz.

Now he sounds upset with the person on the other end of the call.

"You worry about that press conference, and I'll worry about keeping myself out of trouble with Father."

The call ends; the stranger stands and vanishes. I choke on a sort of silent yelp. People vanishing into thin air is one of those things I will *never* get used to. I steady myself and get ready to sprint to the front of the castle.

There's a split-second where I worry about whether or not I will be seen by this invisible person. But if it comes down to hiding here or running to warn my friends and family, I am running.

In the past week, I've gotten badly out of shape. My lungs burn and my calves feel rubbery and then, just as I round the corner of the building, I hit a *wall*. At least that is what it feels like. It takes me a second to realize I've been grabbed by someone who wasn't there a moment ago.

"Really?" I shout, I writhe, and I think I swear. Because I now have concrete evidence that what you

55

can't see *can* hurt you. Of course, now, I can see him just fine.

"Let go of me," I shout. Then I add, "You shouldn't be here!" Which sounds completely lame.

"On the contrary, my dear Miss ... what is it? Li, I believe? I belong here at my father's castle, but I think Father won't be pleased to know *you* are outside."

He grabs my hair, pulling my head around to face his. I can smell his stale coffee breath. He smiles, the kind of smile that is a threat and not a peace treaty.

I squirm again. He's not all that large, or all that strong. If I can get myself to a better position, I can take him on.

"Hold still!" he shouts.

"Not ... a ... chance, Fritz," I say, still struggling.

"You've heard of me," he says, pleased in a way that looks particularly idiotic. I can see his profile: yellowy-gray hair that was probably very blond once. Narrowed eyes, ice-blue, permanent frown lines. An older, less dashing version of Hans. I shudder as the winds roars through the tree branches overhead. My stomach clenches, but I push back at my fear. Hard.

"I am, indeed, Fritz Gottlieb von Helmann," he says. "I'm glad you've heard of me. And I've heard of you, too. Now that we've gone through the pleasantries, why not tell me what Gwyneth Li is doing out here instead of in there?"

"She's about to *Miss Congeniality* you is what she's doing!" The wind howls, blowing my voice back in my face.

"About to *what?*" asks my captor.

I shift one elbow forward, aim for his solar plexus and shout, "Sandra Bullock in *Miss Congeniality*—ever heard of it?"

In a spectacular display of cowardice, he disappears before I can connect. The wind gusts again, shivering the high branches against one another. I aim for the castle once more, shouting for help as I run. This time, Fritz ripples solid only long enough to ram into me so that I stumble, still fifteen feet short of the front door, and then he's gone. I can feel gravel digging through my new jeans and into my knees. I don't feel anything on my palms for a few seconds, which I know is a bad sign. And then I do feel it: hot, stinging pain where the gravel bit into the fleshy part of my palms.

"Coward!" I shout.

A few feet in front of me, Fritz ripples solid again, a gun in his hand. He points it at me.

"You're going to be in so much trouble if you shoot me," I say. "You have no idea how much trouble." My knees and hands are *screaming* at me right now as I hunker on the ground.

For some reason, my warning seems to carry weight with him. He frowns as if to consider what I've said.

"Inside, then," he says. "Get up. In you go."

"With pleasure," I say. Which is an exaggeration of stellar proportion. What I'm feeling at the moment is the opposite of pleasure. My palms feel like I used Ma's microplaner on them, and my knees aren't much better. I am attempting to rise with dignity when the front door swings violently open. It's Sir Walter, with Chrétien at his side.

And now things happen in fast forward.

Fritz rushes to where I've managed to stand and grabs me *again*, jabbing the gun into my throat. I hear a tiny click, but I don't feel dead. Just as Fritz is re-capturing me, Chrétien ripples to invisibility. Sir Walter, seeing the weapon connect to my neck, shouts, "Wait," to the empty spot where Chrétien used to be. But Chrétien is solid at my side a second later, bashing Fritz's gun-wielding hand in such a way that the gun is no longer pointed at me.

It does, however, fire, making it more likely I'll be learning sign language; I can't hear anything for several seconds. As I take in my hearing loss, it occurs to me the tiny click was Fritz releasing the gun's safety. And this just infuriates me.

I shout at him. "You were actually going to *shoot* me! How dare you!" I slam my heel into his instep and he grunts in a way I find quite satisfying. The sound also tells me I'm not permanently deaf.

I'm about to aim one at his *cojones*, but Chrétien does a neat little twist that lands Fritz face first with both arms behind him onto the hood and windshield of Sir Walter's blue Alfa Romeo *Giulietta*.

Chapter Six

THE CASTLE IS MINE

"What do you think you're doing here?" demands Sir Walter.

"Me? What am *I* doing here?" replies Fritz.

"I heard my question the first time I asked it," says Sir Walter. "Did you?"

Fritz sputters, maybe curses under his breath. "I have every right to be here. So far as I know, *you* do not. You will allow me to pass and enter at once."

"That will not be possible," says Chrétien. His voice is velvet-y and dangerous, the voice of a predator.

I take calming breaths and force myself to stand straight and tall. Well, as tall as sixty-one inches gets you. My hands form fists at my side and I run through Sandra Bullock's self-defense moves in my mind.

"What do you mean *'that will not be possible'*?" demands Fritz.

"Your repetition of things already spoken grows wearisome," says Sir Walter.

"Do you know who I am?" asks Fritz.

"Of course, cousin," says Sir Walter. "Perhaps you have forgotten me, however?" He indicates with a movement of his head that Chrétien should allow Fritz to stand upright.

As soon as Chrétien loosens his hold on Fritz, Fritz reaches in his coat for something—another weapon? But in a flash Sir Walter ripples and reappears with one arm around the intruder's neck, the other forcing his arm into what looks like a super uncomfortable position. I make a mental note to learn that move. Minus the rippling part, anyway.

"Chrétien?" Sir Walter calls calmly. "Would you be so kind?"

Chrétien injects Fritz in the neck with a syringe.

I gasp and then cover my mouth. I don't like Fritz, but I really don't care to watch someone die in front of my eyes, either. Chrétien hears my gasp and his eyes find mine. He nods reassuringly. The injection wasn't lethal. I know somehow. In fact, it doesn't appear to be affecting Fritz in any way whatsoever.

"I believe you are familiar with the drug Neuroplex?" Sir Walter asks Fritz.

"This man was the inventor of the anti-rippling tonic, *mon père*," says Chrétien. "You are Dr. Fritz Gottlieb, are you not?"

"How dare you inject *me* with Neuroplex?" wheezes Fritz.

Sir Walter eases off on the neck-lock.

"I have dared a great deal more these past weeks," replies Sir Walter. "Chrétien, remove from this person any further weapons."

"And car keys," I say. "Is that your black sedan at the entrance of the drive?"

"I'll report you for theft," snaps Fritz.

"My dear cousin," says Sir Walter. "I have no interest in stealing your car. I merely wish to prevent you from leaving by a conventional means until we have had a civilized conversation."

Fritz rubs the injection spot on his neck as Chrétien pats him down for further weapons. An ugly knife and a pair of syringes join the revolver, now in Chrétien's care.

Eyeing one of the syringes with longing, Fritz says, "I have more of the Neuroplex antidote where that came from."

"A reverse anti-serum? Fascinating," says Sir Walter. "Now, then, you may stand beside my vehicle while we conclude our conversation. I should advise against further attacks. You are outnumbered, cousin."

Fritz swears and spits: once at Sir Walter, once at his son. Then he looks up at the second floor windows of the castle. "Where is my father?" he demands.

"Your father is even now adjusting to his extended stay in purgatory, I should think," replies Sir Walter. "Assuming he was not sent straight to *l'Inferne.*"

Fritz inhales sharply. "You … *killed* my father?"

"Between us, his death was accomplished," says Chrétien.

"But … but … where are my brothers? What have you done with Hans? With Pfeffer? Where is Franz?" Fritz is scared now. His voice gives him away even though he stands straight as an arrow, his chin and nose aimed high.

"They are gone as well," says Sir Walter.

This isn't entirely true. Pfeffer's south of Paris, last I heard.

"Pfeffer's alive," shouts Fritz, pointing his index finger at Sir Walter and Chrétien in turn. "He responded to an email."

Sir Walter sighs and rubs his eyes. "I believe he told you to cease your attempts to contact him, did he not?"

Fritz frowns. He doesn't deny it.

"Pfeffer lives, but he is not your ally," continues Sir Walter. "So long as you pursue your father's work, we are not your friends, either. Do I make myself clear?"

Fritz glowers.

It is silent except for the wind moaning around the *château* and among the tree tops.

Fritz speaks again. "Am I to understand Franz and Hans are dead?"

"They are, God rest their souls," says Sir Walter, crossing himself.

Chrétien crosses himself, too.

"I see," says Fritz. He brushes his hands along his suit, straightening, tidying.

"Don't try it," warns Sir Walter.

I look, but I can't see any sign Fritz was going to do anything.

"Try what, dear cousin?" asks Fritz, a tiny smile smudging his face. He holds his hands out, demonstrating innocence.

"We overhear your thoughts," says Chrétien.

Fritz swears and his eyes widen. "Father said that was impossible: one of your lies."

"It is no lie," says Sir Walter. "Helmann was a fool about many things."

"On that we are agreed," mutters Fritz.

"I suggest you depart," says Sir Walter.

"If Father is dead, the castle is mine," says Fritz.

"But we hold it," says Chrétien. "Depart, while the opportunity presents itself."

"I have questions—"

"I am not at present inclined to provide answers," says Sir Walter, cutting Fritz off. "I suggest once more that you leave *now*."

"Or what? You'll kill me, too?" asks Fritz. "You're no better than Father was, old man."

"We live, all of us, in hope of redemption," says Sir Walter.

"Bah!" replies Fritz.

Sir Walter nods to Chrétien, who tosses the car key back to Fritz. Fritz catches it, straightens his tie, and turns to leave down the drive. His angry steps toss loose gravel as he goes.

"I do not like his thoughts," says Sir Walter.

"Nor do I," says Chrétien.

"We must depart as soon as may be," says Sir Walter. "Let us warn the others."

Chapter Seven

I'M HEARING VOICES

Chrétien stands to one side of the *château*'s impressive front doors, allowing me and Sir Walter to enter first. The three of us climb the worn marble stairs. My legs have this jittery feeling like I just competed in cross country. I have a flashback to the first time I climbed this staircase, when Hans brought me here. And suddenly, I'm glad we're leaving.

Beside me, Sir Walter sighs gently. "What heavenly scent is this?"

It takes me a minute to place what he's talking about because the smell is one I'm used to breathing pretty much twenty-four seven in Las Abs. It's the smell of Ma's chocolate chip cookies—the ones I'm not allowed to eat unless there are leftovers at the end of the day. Which happens, like, never.

"Ma's cookies," I say. "Hey, about telling my mom what just went down, could we maybe … not?"

Sir Walter pauses on the top step before the oaken door leading into the great hall.

"*Mademoiselle?*" he says softly.

"Just … please don't mention the … fight. Or the survival of a Hans-sibling to Ma," I say. "She'll freak. She's been through enough already."

Honestly, I haven't been doing anything to help in that area. I shove my hands deep in my pockets and resolve for the gazillionth time to be a better daughter.

"Indeed," says Sir Walter. "Let us not alarm your dear mother." He smiles, puts one hand on goatee-duty. "But I judge it would be best if we departed within the hour."

We push through the heavy door. After the chill of the outdoors, it feels like a sauna in here. And the smell of baking brown sugar, butter, and chocolate—Ma's alchemical equation—is overwhelming.

"Chocolate chip cookies," says Will. He's grinning ear to ear, but then, seeing our expressions, he frowns. "Was there a problem outside?"

Sir Walter tells Will and Sam about our encounter with Fritz.

"I'll tell Ma we're leaving," I say.

"Tell her to pack the cookies," says Will. "Do you know how long it's been since I've had a chocolate chip cookie?"

I give him a strained smile. "Sure."

Sir Walter leaves to pack up his stuff, and Sam

66

and Will are heading off, too.

I sigh and walk to the kitchen. From the corner of my eye, I see Chrétien hesitate before the fireplace and then follow me. No idea why, other than the lure of Ma's cookies. My mind flashes back to the day Chrétien, Sam, and I made cookies at Sam's house, and Chrétien flipped over the taste. I remember chasing Chrétien around the pool with half a bag of flour. Before Hans burned Sam's house to the ground.

It feels like it happened a lifetime ago. To someone else.

"Hey, Ma," I say as I walk in.

"You're back," Ma says, inspecting my new jeans, my red shoes. "Those jeans are too tight. You'll have to take them back."

"Can't," I say. "They don't have American refund policies in France."

Ma frowns and says a few things in Chinese about my backside attracting more attention than a backside should attract.

"The cookies smell good," I say, so Ma stops nattering on about my backside.

"They're … different," she says. "French ingredients, I suppose."

I nod and run my index finger through a dusting of flour on the counter, exposing the ancient white marble, veined with gray and black. I'm working up to telling Ma the news in a way that doesn't scare her.

"So," I say, "it turns out we need to leave. Now."

"Your passport came already? That's impossible."

67

"No. Not that kind of leave. I still don't have my passport. We're leaving the *château*, not France."

"Oh, are we?" Ma's face brightens. "How wonderful." She hugs me, whispering, "Is this your doing? Thank you so much."

"Um," I say, but I don't add anything else. I guess I can let her think it's my doing.

"The cookies, though...." Ma looks a bit distressed. "You know how I feel about leftover dough."

"Ruins the crumb. Got it, Ma. We can make more at the new place," I say.

A timer sounds on Ma's phone and she turns swiftly to the oven. At home, burnt cookies mean money down the drain.

"The kitchen doesn't have cooling racks," Ma says, "but the counters are marble, which should cool them fast."

I note Chrétien's focus on the cookies and pass him one. "Have a taste," I say. *Of, you know, the cookies, my lips, whatever.*

I so need to find another dude to crush on. I turn and look away.

Sir Walter strides in the kitchen just then. "My dear *Madame* Li, you have quite outdone yourself."

Ma makes a *phhht* noise. "I could make this recipe in my sleep. In fact, I think I have."

Sam and Will trail Sir Walter into the kitchen.

"You guys ready already?" I ask.

"Mmm-hmm," says Sam, hastily wiping at a

smudge on Will's cheek.

Her lip gloss.

I hate my life.

Ten minutes later, freshly baked chocolate chip cookies bagged up, we are ready to say *au revoir* to Château Feu-Froid.

"How far away is the new place?" Ma asks, yawning widely behind one flour-specked hand. "I could use a nap."

"What is our, how do you say, our *destination?*" Chrétien asks Sir Walter.

"Destination," we all (except Ma) say together.

Chrétien's high-boned cheeks flush rosy pink. Oh, the moisturizer you could sell with that face. If dudes bought moisturizer.

"We travel to the south," Sir Walter says vaguely. "Plenty of time for a cat-nap, *Madame* Li."

"You told Mick and Pfeffer where to find us, right?" asks Will as we make our way to Sir Walter's car.

"They are informed in that regard," says Sir Walter. "We will be considerably nearer them, as it happens."

Sir Walter explains we're heading for his place in the south of France. At first I'm thinking it's another castle, but as they discuss who will sleep where, it sounds more like they're discussing an old farmhouse. Will is offering to sleep invisibly, in the walls.

This makes Ma shudder and shake her head.

"No, no, my friend," says Sir Walter to Will. "You

have a broken limb to mend. No time off for you."

Sam explains to me and Ma that if Will is invisible, his body goes into a hibernating state where nothing changes, hence, nothing heals. And now all the ripplers are arguing over who gets to sleep invisibly, which, is just ... wrong. How is it I got roped into this crowd?

The topic comes up again when the six of us stare into Sir Walter's car which only has four seatbelts.

"In truth," says Chrétien, "we can travel more comfortably if two do so without substance."

"Not me," says my ma. "Sorry, but I've had enough rippling to last a lifetime."

"It cannot be myself, as I must drive," says Sir Walter.

"I'll ripple," says Will. "With Sam."

"You'll stay in the car and heal is what you'll do," says Sam.

"I will travel insubstantially," says Chrétien.

"I get carsick," I say. "Is there any chance that would go away if I was ... invisible?" I remember something about Sam saying she's never cold or hungry when she ripples.

"You can't feel carsick when you're invisible," says Will.

Another minute of discussion and it is decided: Chrétien will carry me into ripple-world, and the rest will ride in the car.

Ma is muttering under her breath.

"It's okay, Ma, really," I say, planting a tiny kiss

on one of her cheeks.

She looks at me, worried, and nods.

"So how do we do this?" I ask Chrétien.

His cheeks pop out bright pink spots again as he explains. "I believe I must ... enfold you within my grasp."

This, it turns out, means we hold hands, which is not nearly as much enfolding as I might have been hoping for. Still, his hand in mine is warm, and in the two perfect seconds it takes Chrétien to disappear, I smell something warm and spicy along with a hint of chocolate chip cookie. And then I don't smell anything. I'm invisible. Inside a car.

"Oh," says Sam, buckling up just after I disappear. "I came up with the perfect topic for you, Gwyn. For that French paper."

Can't talk right now, Sam. Invisible and all.

Chrétien laughs.

Wait. I *heard* that. I heard Chrétien laughing, I swear.

Dude, I think, *did you just laugh?*

And what do I hear in my head? A spoken "yes," in Chrétien's voice.

Oh, this is great. Just great. *I'm hearing voices.*

Chapter Eight

BALLET IS FOR DUDES

You are not hearing voices, says Chrétien. *You are hearing* my *voice. Well, and that of your friend* Mademoiselle *Samantha.*

This is true. Sam is still talking, because apparently she can't hear Chrétien and *moi* having our little *tête-à-tête*.

"So, you know," Sam says, "considering how you watch all those dance shows, I think it would be perfect. And Chrétien can tell you all about Louis Quatorze and dancing," concludes Sam.

Of what am I to speak to you? asks Chrétien. *Of dancing?*

Um, I reply, *Sam must be talking about the assignment for French class. I'm supposed to write a four page paper about some aspect of Le Roi-Soleil, Louis the Fourteenth of France.*

72

Ah, Chrétien responds. *And this project can be upon the topic of dancing?*

Yup. So long as it is Louis-related.

Chrétien laughs again. *Do you know, Mademoiselle, under whose reign I passed my youth?*

Will said something about you being born the same year as the Sun King, I say. *Is that true?*

Indeed, replies Chrétien. *From my fifteenth year, I passed my time as a member of his court.*

Seriously?

Truly, replies Chrétien. And I can actually feel a tiny bit of his emotion: delight. Enough that I know what the expression on his face would be right now.

Which brings up a few questions about how we are … communicating.

Wait a minute, wait a minute, I say, half to Chrétien, half to myself. *How come I can hear what you are thinking, but I couldn't hear what The Hans and Franz Show were thinking?*

The Hans and Franz show? Chrétien sounds puzzled. I can just picture his brows pulling together.

Oh, sorry. That's what I called the guys who held me hostage at the castle, I explain. *At different times, each of them rippled me invisible with them. Hans abducted me first, but Franz grabbed me in France, when I tried to run. And I never heard them in my head.*

Not once? asks Chrétien.

Never. Not that I would have wanted to. Ick!

As to the why … we shall have to consult Sir Walter. I can only say they have no drop of de Rochefort blood within them.

Dude! I reply. *Asian here. Pretty sure there's no de Rochefort in me, either.*

Chrétien laughs. *As I said, we must consult* mon père, *my father.*

At that moment, however, something occurs to me. Now I'm worried. Can Chrétien hear all my thoughts? *Did you just hear me think that, um, I'm worried about something?* I ask Chrétien.

I did not. If our communication is like that I have shared with others, I will hear only what you intend for me.

THANK GOODNESS, I think to myself.

This falls into a category of issues of which my father often speaks, muses Chrétien.

No clue how I know he's musing. I just do.

When he trained me as a chameleon—a rippler— my father reported unto me that with many things, it is our intention that matters most.

Intention matters most? The heck? *What is that supposed to mean?* I ask.

Well, replies Chrétien, *suppose you wish to keep some of your thoughts to yourself. You can do so by not intending them for me.*

Right. Got it.

With motion, continues Chrétien, *my father trained me early that to desire a motion is the same as achieving it. That is, have you considered how it is that we remain within the walls of this horseless carriage?*

I can't say I've considered it. Not remotely. *No,* I respond.

Well, if I wished, I could take us out through the roof of the carriage. Or plunge us down beneath the passageway upon which we speed.

Ugh! No! Don't you dare do either of those things!

I hear Chrétien's laughter inside my mind.

Have no fear, Mademoiselle. I do not desire to do so either, and so long as it is not part of my intent, it will not be part of our experience, either.

I think about this for a few seconds. *That's just weird.*

Not at all, argues Chrétien. *Think of yourself as in a stream of water. Imagine it as of a depth sufficient that you could, if you so desired, plunge yourself underwater. Now imagine instead that you are carried by the stream, that you make no effort to move of your own accord.*

So, rippling is like being in a stream? I ask.

Well, it is not a perfect analogy, but there are similarities. You can choose to plunge under water or to rise out of it, can you not?

Yeah, I answer. *I guess so. Although, if you were unconscious, you wouldn't be doing much swimming. The stream would just carry you.*

Chrétien is silent for a moment. *I believe the analogy would still hold true. An unconscious cham—er, rippler— would not, lacking intention, have governance of his motion, either.*

So don't go unconscious on me, okay?

His laughter fills my mind. *Allow not yourself to worry.*

Right, I respond. *Because that's so easy when I'm*

75

freaking invisible!

Might I, asks Chrétien, *tell you* une histoire—*a story? Would you like that?*

Um, sure? A story would definitely take my mind off my disturbing lack of substance.

Such was my intention, says Chrétien. And he launches into his tale with the best four words to start any story.

Once upon a time, there was a very young prince whose father fell ill and died. The reine, *the queen, loved her little boy very much. But she knew that many of the nobles of the land would like to prevent the boy from growing to an age where he could assume the crown, as they thought they might wear it better themselves.*

In this environment of threat, the boy grew under the care of his mother. She taught him to love les beaux arts: *drawing, music, theater, and dance. And of course she taught him as well to consign his fate into the care of Most Holy God. After all, as God had seen fit to bring the boy into his mother's womb after a twenty years barren marriage, surely God had plans for the young king's good.*

However, often it seemed as if Most Holy God had forgotten the prince. His countrymen fought amongst themselves and attacked the minister who ran the country on the child-king's behalf, and before he had reached ten years of age, the boy had known both poverty and starvation. But in his tenth year, peace was restored to his land, and he began to live more after the fashion of a prince.

His education, besides his religious instruction, included history, politics, some economics, and always, there was the theatre, dance, and la musique.

I interrupt. *Is this a true story?*

Chrétien's laughter rings in my head. *As true as truth*, he says.

Is it the story of your life? I ask next.

My life? No, no, no. Again with the laughter. *This is the story of Louis Quatorze, the Sun King. Upon whom you are commanded to create a composition, if I am not mistaken.*

I sigh. *You're not mistaken. Any idea why Sam thinks I should do a paper on dancing?*

But of course, replies Chrétien, *the Sun King was a most passionate advocate of the dance, which was called at the time* "le ballet."

I interrupt. *"Ballet" as in ... ballet?*

Do you inquire so as to determine if the word is the same in French and English?

Um, yeah.

Yes, I believe the word is the same, Chrétien replies.

Okay, so this starving king was big on ballet? I ask.

But of course, replies Chrétien. *Ballet saved the kingdom.*

Ballet? Saved France? I find that hard to believe.

Nevertheless, replies Chrétien, *it is so. The French kings recognized the power of spectacle to assuage the passions ... to calm the violence within man, and thus, to prevent its eruption between those who disputed.*

Huh. I am pretty sure this wouldn't succeed in today's world. *Did it work?*

Mademoiselle, *you sound as though you had doubts. Have you never observed the power of a song, of a dance, to soothe the savage nature of man?*

I think for a minute. I mean, sure, I've heard the saying, "Music soothes the savage beast," but I sort of thought the saying was about, I don't know, lions and tigers and bears. On the other hand, I have had some firsthand experience with being soothed by music myself, or being moved by watching a couple dance with everything they have to give.

Is not music a reflection of the order of the universe? asks Chrétien.

I thought the universe was in a state of increasing chaos, I reply.

Given such a belief, responds Chrétien, *it is no wonder the arts have no hope of bringing peace into the world you inhabit.*

It sounds depressing when you put it like that, I admit.

Chrétien is silent for a full minute this time.

I am just deciding he's done talking when, finally, I hear him again. *There are aspects of living in your time which I find troublesome. Perhaps your world has, indeed, lost the ability to feel the soothing power of the arts.*

We're both quiet for a long time. I think through the things he's said and try to imagine a world where the universe is seen as orderly. And honestly, even though I said something about the chaotic nature of the universe, I don't really know what it means. I was just parroting something from a physics paper one of my old boyfriends had me edit for grammar.

I mean, when I think about the world, sure, crazy-mad chaos is everywhere. But when I think about the universe—like, the stars, the moon, the sun—I guess I'd have to say that from where I'm standing, I see a bunch of order. I get a full moon once a month whether I need it or not, and the Little Dipper spins around the North Star year in and year out. Orderly. Repeated. Reliable. Even the strange stuff like meteor showers and comets and eclipses can be predicted.

And then something comes back to me, and I want to tell Chrétien about it.

You still there? I ask Chrétien.

I have not departed, he replies.

It's just … I thought of something. I saw a live flash mob two years ago.

Chrétien is silent for several seconds. *I am unfamiliar with the words you employ.*

Sorry, I say. *Yeah, I think flash mobs are pretty modern. It's when a group of people sing or play music or dance or all three together.*

A concert? asks Chrétien.

Sort of. Only, the audience doesn't know it's going to happen.

Chrétien asks, *How is it possible to assemble an audience without their knowledge?*

I laugh. Or … whatever you do invisibly when something's funny. *That's the point. Flash mobs don't happen in theaters or on stages. People do them in shopping malls or Time Square or Red Square. Where no one's expecting them, right in the middle of an ordinary place. First one person starts the performance and then people join in, like they're coming out of the woodwork, you see?*

An individual coerces a group to join him in performing? asks Chrétien. *Without rehearsal? The performance cannot be of very high quality, in such a case.*

No, no, I say. *The ones who join have all rehearsed together. Lots of rehearsing together. Then they show up and surprise people with a performance.*

Ah, says Chrétien. *What a noble endeavor.*

Um, yeah, actually, I reply.

May I ask what made you wish to explain unto me the … flash mobbing?

Flash mob, I say. *Well, the year Ma and I left Los Angeles for good, there was a shooting at the mall where Ma ran one of the aunties' bakeries. I was there helping in the back, so I missed seeing the bad stuff, but what I heard was awful enough.* I pause. *People died.*

I am sorry Mademoiselle *had to experience such a thing.*

Yeah, I say. Mademoiselle*'s sorry, too. But the reason I told you about it is that, maybe a week or so later, a flash mob gathered in our mall and played Beethoven's Ode to Joy. Now, I'm not a Beethoven kind of girl, Chrétien. I didn't even know it was Beethoven at the time. But here's what I do know. After the shooting, our little shopping mall felt full of death and hopelessness. It was a dark place. But that orchestra or whatever they called themselves brought hope back inside our mall.*

You could see it in people's faces when they stopped shopping and just listened. A ton of people cried. Didn't even try to hide it. Mostly people smiled. Kids danced and copied the conductor, waving their arms all over. It was like the whole mall started breathing again. I pause for a few seconds. *I don't know if that makes much sense.*

It sounds to me, Chrétien replies, *as though order was restored to your, how do you say? Corner of the universe?*

Yeah, I say. *Like that thing you said earlier about the power of spectacle ... something or other.*

The power of spectacle to assuage the passions, says Chrétien. *Perhaps your world is not so different from mine of old.*

Maybe, huh? I'm glad I told him. I haven't even told Sam about the mall shooting. Even though that's what made Ma decide we were moving back to Las Abuelitas for good.

So, I say, *tell me more about ballet. I think I might do my paper on Louis the Fourteenth: Dancing with the Stars.*

Dancing with the Stars, Mademoiselle?

Never mind, I reply. *Just tell me about ballet back in the day.*

Chrétien pauses. *About which aspect of the dance do you wish to be informed?*

Um ... I don't know. Start at the beginning, maybe. How old would I be if I were learning to dance in the ... uh ... whatever century we're talking about.

You, Mademoiselle?

Yeah. Me. If I lived back then, what age would I start taking ballet lessons?

You are the female of the species.

Yeah. No kidding. I mean, about time he notice, and all, but I'm not seeing the relevance. *And your point is....?*

Le Ballet is for ... was for men, replies Chrétien.

What? Ballet? For dudes? Since when?

81

Chrétien sounds confused. *If we are to speak of the age of Louis Quatorze, then ballet would be the province of men, naturally. Although I am informed this has changed in the intervening centuries.*

Yeah, I reply, *a lot must have changed. Are you telling me guys dressed up in frilly white tutus and pointe shoes in your era?*

I am not familiar with the "tutus" or the "pointe shoes," Chrétien replies. *But I assure you it is most natural that ballet was the province of men. Women went not to war in my time, and you must understand,* Mademoiselle, *that dance has its roots in the martial arts, along with riding horseback and the use of arms, that is, weaponry. Dance was taught to boys of noble birth from the time they could walk, ride, and hold a sword.*

Ballet for boys. Weird. Although I guess they call it choreography in film whether it's fighting or dancing.

Chrétien continues. *To dance well is simply to present one's body in the most pleasing and perfect way at all times, whether passing a superior in a hall, or engaging an enemy with the sword, or performing to the accompaniment of music.*

Well, I can definitely attest to the fact that Chrétien's body is "at all times" *highly* pleasing, so maybe the French had something after all. I don't say this to Chrétien, of course.

Okay, so ballet was just for guys in the time of Louis. Got it. So, is this like where dudes go in drag as girls? Like Shakespeare?

"In drag"? asks Chrétien.

Sorry. It means, dressed as girls. Cross-dressing. That's what they did when Shakespeare was alive. At least according to my English teacher.

Your professeur of English is correct. Both upon the English and the French stage, the parts of women were enacted by men for public performances. Troupes of actors who performed for private engagements might include girls and women. However, it was not considered seemly for a woman to appear upon a public stage, so the roles of women were undertaken by men. Louis himself was a notably attractive shepherdess upon one occasion in my recollection.

I laugh. *You got to love a ruler who doesn't take himself too seriously.*

Hmm, Chrétien replies. *I would not wish to imply that my king took himself less than completely seriously at all times. In fact, I recollect his saying once, "They are mistaken who believe* l'etiquette *is mere ceremony and* la danse *an entertainment."*

"Etiquette" as in "etiquette?" I ask. *Where to put your napkin when you're done with dinner?*

Chrétien laughs. *Etiquette is the cousin of* le ballet, *encompassing all action, including the proper placement of one's napkin after dinner. It includes as well how it is proper to approach the king, how to depart from his presence, where to allow one's glance to fall, how to turn one's wrist when playing a game of tennis. Oh,* Mademoiselle, l'etiquette *formed the all-in-all of my life at court. None of this could I have mastered without training in the art of the dance.*

Wow, I say. *This is going to be more than a four page paper. I am so getting extra credit in French. So, in summary, boys start military dancing lessons as soon as they can walk; all movement is governed by these lessons; no girls allowed in ballet performances. Does that about sum it up?*

There was a girl, says Chrétien, *once there was a girl.*

I wait to see if he's going to add anything to this. His tone's a bit ominous. Or angsty, maybe. Although, I have no idea how I'm getting ominous-slash-angsty given that this is all just voices in my head.

Ah, says Chrétien, in a very non-angsty way. *We approach now the lands of my father's* famille—*my father's family.*

I take a look out the windows. During our drive, the land has changed from rolling fields to these pretty intense mountain-y stretches that sort of remind me of the road from Mariposa to Yosemite. The same low ground cover, green, and the same steep slopes. Not exactly mountains, by California standards, but pretty mountainous, anyway.

And then, on one of the hills, I spot a ruined castle. It is beautiful in a way that sort of breaks your heart. Even more than the abandoned side yard back at Château Feu-Froid.

Look! I call to Chrétien.

There are many such ruins in this region, Chrétien tells me. *My father's own castle is one such. It is …* triste.

Sad, I say. *I know.*

Now Sir Walter is talking, waking up Ma, and pointing out some gravel road to Sam and Will. I guess I'm out of time to ask about the "once there was a girl" business.

84

We pull onto a side road that turns out to be the private driveway leading to Sir Walter's little cottage in the south of France.

"Hey," says Will. "What's with the front door?"

I look over to the front door of the tidy white-washed farmhouse. It's wide open.

"Someone is here," says Sir Walter. "Chrétien, come with me. Remain in your chameleon form." Then he turns and addresses Sam and Will. "Ree-pill to safety with *Madame* Li."

And he opens the car door, steps out, and ripples invisible.

Chapter Nine

A TYLENOL OF THE HEART

Okay, so one of the weirder features of being invisible? Your heartbeat. You don't have one. I mean, mine should be thumping like crazy in my ribcage right now.

Chrétien, are you scared? I ask.

That is a difficult state to achieve whilst incorporeal, he replies.

He's right. I try real hard to feel afraid as we head toward the house. I'm guessing Chrétien is the one doing the heading—I'm just sort of hanging on to him like a sweater he's wearing. Mmm. There's something I'd like to be: the clothes he wears everyday.

Gwyn. Stop it.

I don't get to be Chrétien's sweater. I don't get to be his anything. Sir Walter made that clear. And now I discover it is possible to feel heartache without a beating heart.

I will allow no ill to befall you, Mademoiselle *Gwyn,* says Chrétien.

Yeah. Except for the part where you make yourself irresistible as Ma's cookies and unavailable as syllaberries in winter.

Then I realize I am hearing a convo in French between Sir Walter and his son.

Sir Walter? I say. *I can hear you, too?*

Evidently you can, replies Sir Walter. *Fascinating. Chrétien, my son, was it difficult to establish contact with* Mademoiselle's *mind?*

No, indeed, replies Chrétien.

Most fascinating, says Sir Walter. *We must speak of this when we are less ... occupied.*

Chrétien and I follow Sir Walter through the open door and then through each room, one by one. Sir Walter and Chrétien have switched to English, so I don't feel left out, I assume. I just listen and ... cling. Or whatever this is.

At one point, Chrétien slides through a wall instead of stepping out into the hallway. Which is just ... freakazoidal. While we are inside the wall, I can't see anything for a second, and I feel like I'm getting tickled, and then we push through into a room, and I can see again.

A little warning, next time, maybe? I ask.

I beg pardon, Mademoiselle. *I am accustomed to considering only my own wishes whilst incorporeal. I shall not pass through walls if* Mademoiselle *would prefer.*

Um, yeah, Mademoiselle *would definitely prefer.*

From somewhere, outside maybe, I catch a thumping noise. It sounds like someone's getting their backside handed to them on a platter.

Chrétien? That sound?

Chrétien zips us through the exterior wall of the farmhouse—*Ew!*—to where the sound is coming from.

My jaw would drop right now if I had one. The 'beating' sound we heard is a very old, very thin woman *thwapping* a hanging rug for all she's worth.

I hear Chrétien's sigh of relief. *The housekeeper*, he says to me. He calls to his dad, relaying the good news. A second later, Sir Walter, now solid, comes from around the front of the house and greets the old woman in something not quite French. Spanish, maybe?

Chrétien walks us back around the building, taking into consideration my preference for avoiding rippling through solid walls. Then he seems to hesitate.

What's wrong? I ask.

I am merely ascertaining no part of your body is currently within any solid object.

Oh. Right. Sam gave me a play by play of a couple of her misadventures in that area. I don't want to experience it firsthand.

Rejoining the land of solid objects means I have to let go of Gorgeous. Which I manage, in spite of how he smells like exotic spices and warm chocolate chip cookies.

"Thank you, *Mademoiselle*, for allowing me to shield you," says Chrétien.

His voice sounds funny coming from outside of me. Disappointing. Or like that moment where you wake up with your blanket on the floor and you're all cold and miserable.

"No, really, it was my pleasure," I say. Even though I shouldn't say things like that. This boy is a fever I have got to get over.

I wonder if anyone has considered inventing a Tylenol of the heart?

I turn and crunch through powdery gravel to rejoin Ma and the others. Of course, they are invisible at the moment, and I have to admit I feel pretty stupid when I speak to an empty car.

"Everything's fine," I say. "It's someone who comes to clean for Sir Walter once a month."

Will zips back solid with my mom holding his hand. She shakes her head several times, looking about as happy as a wet cat. Beside them, Sam reappears, smiling at the farmhouse like it's full of good memories. I guess it is—this was where she and Will declared their undying love or something equally depressing.

I sigh and head back to the house, my body *solid* this time.

Behind me, Ma's cell jingles and she answers it, remaining outside. She's been taking calls all day, about where to find stuff in the bakery, mostly.

Apparently the aunties think she should have stuck to the organizational system they had in LA. Ma switches from Cantonese dialect to Mandarin. I know a little Cantonese from growing up around it at home, but I know almost no Mandarin, apart from a few swear words, so Ma and her sisters speak Mandarin when they want to hide stuff from me.

I cross the threshold. In my pocket, my cell vibes, too. It's a text. José from cross country.

When are you coming back? AP Biology is bogus without your jokes.

I smile. Someone appreciates my jokes. Unfortunately, the someone in this case appreciates my everything. This would be great if I felt even a little bit of a spark between us. Sadly, I don't.

"Who is it?" asks Sam, dumping her bag on the farmhouse table in the kitchen.

"José," I reply.

"Someone misses you," she says.

I groan.

"Someone thinks you're hot," says Will to me.

"I know," I say, miserably.

My cell buzzes again.

You still owe me a date.

Sam reads the text over my shoulder and grins. "Looks like Will is right on that score."

"It's all my fault. I might have flirted with José a few times last fall. And maybe this winter. When I was between boy-flings."

"Answer him," says Sam.

CIDNEY SWANSON

I groan again.

Will grabs his bag and Sam's bag and hobbles with them to some other part of the building. I hear him chuckling as he moves down the hall away from us.

"Are you going to ignore José?" asks Sam.

"Is that an option?" I reply.

"No. That would be rude."

"I'm a rude human being," I say. "Ask my mom."

Sam shakes her head at me, sighing.

I sink into a chair at the table and bury my face in my hands.

"It's my fault," I mumble into my hands. "I might have led him on at your Ground Hog's Eve party. To get Chrétien's attention."

"Gwyneth Li!"

"I'm a horrible person. It's true. I am. José has liked me since I first moved back to Las Abs, and I let him think there was a chance when there's not."

"You're going to text him back right now and tell him you are sorry if you led him to believe you were interested," says Sam.

"Will you text him for me?"

"Gwyn!"

I sit up. Dutifully, I type in more or less what Sam said. And I apologize. This is something new for me—apologizing to a boy for flirting.

"Doesn't that feel better?" asks Sam.

"It feels worse. I feel like a total … *heel.* Is that the word I'm looking for?"

91

"It will do," says Sam. She sits down beside me and puts an arm around me. "Just, you should think a little more before you flip on the high beams, okay? Guys don't stand a chance against you once you turn on the razzle-dazzle." She pauses for a second. "That's why I keep getting in your face about not flirting with Chrétien. He's … fragile. And I don't want to see anything happening to him."

"Sir Walter told me this morning about how he lost everything. I mean, everyone."

"Okay. So long as you know to go easy on him."

I laugh a short harsh laugh. "Trust me, he's not interested."

Sam shrugs.

And, in any case, how I feel about Chrétien is different. I don't know how to explain this to Sam. I've never felt half this strongly about any other guy I've set my sights on. Figures. The one I could actually be serious about isn't available.

José texts me. It is a long text. And rather full of phrases like "heart-breaker" and "leading someone on" and "you should" and "you shouldn't." It's all pretty good advice, actually, but as depressing as discovering you left your window down and it rained all over the driver's seat. I show Sam and she hugs me.

I text back another apology. And then José must have decided I learned my lesson. He types, *We're cool. I mean, let me know if you ever change your mind, obviously.*

I type *okay.*

Sam gives me another hug.

José sends one last text.

Hey, you might want to tell your mom her sisters are making people crazy at the bakery. They keep trying to sell burned cookies and charge for coffee refills and stuff. In case your mom cares.

I sigh. Ma will be so happy to hear this. When Death Valley floods and freezes over. Just then, my mom walks inside the farmhouse, looking it over with her very critical eye.

"Small," she says.

"Ma," I say, rolling my eyes. "A little gratitude?"

Sir Walter must have finished up with his housekeeper outside. He strolls into the house, welcoming us, Chrétien following him inside.

"It is not large or grand," Sir Walter says, "but it has the virtue of being quite secret."

"It's ... lovely," says my mom.

I scrape my jaw off the floor. My mother. Exhibiting gratitude. It's a red letter day for the Li women.

"Wait 'til you see how cozy it is at night, with a fire roaring," says Sam. She clearly thinks this is the last word in vacation homes.

"Yeah," I say. "And no one was drugged or murdered or anything here, right Sir Walter?"

Sam punches my arm, glaring at me. She's right of course. I am a horrible daughter.

I walk over to Ma, apologize in Chinese, and hug her. It takes a second, but she hugs me back.

And then she shakes her head, saying, half to

herself, "What am I going to do about the cats?" She sinks into the couch in the main room.

"What's with the cats?" I ask, determined to devote myself to being a good daughter from now on.

"They're not eating. Woody Allen won't even come out from inside the scratching post hidey-hole."

That's not good. "Woody Allen is claustrophobic," I say. "Maybe the aunties got him confused with someone else?"

"Gwyn, how many albino cats do we have?"

Ma's right. It would be hard to get Woody Allen confused with any of the other fourteen cats at our place.

"And Jet Li is fighting with the other boys," Ma adds.

"That's hardly a surprise," I say.

Ma shrugs.

"Who's not eating?" I ask.

"My sisters aren't sure. Most of the kennels have leftover kibble each morning."

"They miss us," I say.

Ma bunches her hands into tight fists.

"It'll be okay," I say. "They'll survive." But then I remember José's text. "Oh. There's something I should probably pass on to you." Quickly, I list the complaints José told me about.

Which occasions a round of swearing in Mandarin.

"I know those words, Ma."

She puts a hand to her mouth.

I don't know which words mean which body parts and actions, precisely, but Ma doesn't need to know that.

"This is terrible," she says. "I've got to go home."

I frown. "It's just a few more days."

"We don't know that," says my mom. "You heard Sir Walter. We could be stuck here for weeks." She starts to tear up. I hate when Ma cries.

But she's right. France isn't going to stop being France anytime soon. We could be stuck here awhile.

"You could go without me, you know," I say, wrapping an arm around her shoulders. "It would be okay."

"No, it wouldn't," she says, shaking her head through her tears. "Someone's got to take care of you."

"Ma, don't be silly."

"I'm not being silly," she insists. "I let my guard down for ten minutes back home and look what almost happened." She dries her eyes as a few more tears sneak out.

"Ma," I say. "You listen to me. That wasn't your fault. And it's not going to happen again. Those guys are all ... out of the picture." In consideration for my mom, I don't say "dead." And I don't mention Fritz.

"Bridget," says Sam, kneeling in front of us and taking one of Ma's hands, "Gwyn would be just fine here, if you felt you should go home. All of us can take care of her."

"Sam's right, Ma," I say. "I have my own personal

army of super heroes here."

Ten minutes later, we have convinced Ma that No One Will Kidnap Her Daughter if she goes home, and an hour later, Sir Walter is taking her to an airport, having booked her a first class seat, non-stop to San Francisco.

Ma and I hug, and I even kiss her on both cheeks, French style. And then Sir Walter's car pulls out of the driveway, crunching over the gravel, and my mom's on her way home.

I sigh and sit down at the kitchen table. And suddenly I am completely exhausted. Like, I just ran a ten-k exhausted.

"I'm calling it a night," I say.

"We have not yet dined," says Chrétien.

"Not hungry," I say. "Just—" A yawn cuts off my words. "Tired. See you all in the morning."

Dragging my tired self back to the bedroom, I crawl in under the covers and I swear I fall asleep before my head hits the pillow.

The next thing I know, morning light is streaming through my window, and Sam is shaking me awake and saying something about how awful it is and poor Chrétien!

Chapter Ten

OVER MY COLD AND DECEASED FLESH

Now, if Ma had the inside scoop on Yours Truly, she would invent an alarm app that said things about "poor Chrétien" in order to get me out of bed in the morning. Sam's got my attention and I sit up.

"What?" I say. At this point I realize I have glued my hair to the side of my face with my own drool. "Gross," I mumble, tugging black strands back behind my ears. "What's wrong with Chrétien? What happened?"

Sam's face is all squinchy and she's doing this thing, almost flapping her hands.

"Sam!" I snap. "What?"

"It's his diary," Sam tells me.

"Chrétien has a diary?"

"No. His wife's diary. The one who died."

Yeah, I was pretty clear which wife we were talking about.

"What happened to his wife's diary?"

"Fritz has it."

"Fritz? Brother of The Hans and Franz Show Fritz?"

Sam nods. "Apparently, after we left, Fritz went back to the *château*. I mean, he must have, because he took Chrétien's wife's journal from there."

"Wait," I say. "Fritz wants the diary of Chrétien's dead wife?"

"No. At least, I don't think so. It sounds like he thought he was getting Helmann's journal. And now he says he wants to do a trade."

"That's not going to happen," I say. "Is it?"

"No," agrees Sam. "Which is what makes it so awful for Chrétien. He'll never see his wife's diary again."

I'm out of bed and down the hall. I don't need to change since I crashed in my clothes anyway. Which reminds me I'm going to need more clothes soon.

As Sam and I walk out to the main room, I discover a roaring blaze going in the fireplace again. Must be the handiwork of Sir Walter; dude's like, a full on pyromaniac. This is probably a good thing because we didn't have room to pack up the space heaters.

I head for the couch, and I see Chrétien's already there, alone in the room. His body is folded over on itself; his head's resting in his hands, elbows on his knees. He may not be crying, but he's bummed. And something inside me flares like a struck match.

How *dare* someone steal the last connection Chrétien had with the woman he loved?

"Chrétien?" Sam's voice is low, cautious. "Is it okay if we show Gwyn the video?"

Chrétien doesn't respond at first. Then he rises, sighing heavily, and murmurs he has *conceived a desire for fresh air*, or something like that. I want to go after him, but he didn't say he had conceived a desire for Gwyn. Sadly.

Sam sits down at Will's computer and brings up a frozen image of our friend Fritz. He's wearing a very self-satisfied smile.

I shiver and grab the cloak Chrétien sewed from that fire department blanket another lifetime ago in California.

Sam starts the video.

Greetings, my cousins. You have something of my father's and I would like it back. I have something which I imagine you would like to have back as well.

Here Fritz pauses and flips through the pages of a brown leather journal. It's pretty classy looking. Like, if I kept a journal, I would want one like that. Fritz continues.

At first, I was in expectation I had discovered my father's book. Unfortunately, I seem to have mistaken this ... lady's diary for what I desire.

Here Fritz's lips pull back. I think he's trying to grin, but all I see are bared teeth and eyes that look like steel. My stomach growls loudly.

Shall we make a trade? What I have for what I want? You may contact me by return email. I will wait. Let me see ... shall we say forty-eight hours? After that, well ... I like burning things quite as much as did my late brother Hans.

The not-grin slips off his face like soap down the drain.

Oh, and if we cannot reach an agreement with what I have already obtained, I assure you that I have no qualms obtaining other ... things ... you value more highly.

The video ends.

An empty stomach is now the least of my concerns.

"Is he threatening another kidnapping?" I ask, my voice husky.

"Sir Walter thought so," replies Sam. "Although Will was thinking Fritz's use of the word 'things' instead of the word 'people' was encouraging."

I use one of the swear words Ma grounds me for. Sam, who *hates* colorful language, doesn't bat an eye.

"Where are they right now?" I ask. "Will and Sir Walter?"

"They went to secure the journal Sir Walter has and then tell Mick and Pfeffer to keep an extra close eye on the journal they have."

"We have ... two?"

"Yes. One of them has the recordings of all the awful things Helmann did in World War Two. That's with Mick and Pfeffer. So they can explain the truth to the Angel Corps member—the sleepers—they're working with right now. The other is a journal Will and I stole from Helga's office at UC Merced. It has the ..." Here she leans in so she can whisper. "It has the pass phrase that wakes the sleepers up from their hypnotized state."

"Oh," I whisper back. "So, no way Fritz is getting his hands on either one of those, right?"

Sam grunts a short laugh. "As Sir Walter said, 'Over my cold and deceased flesh.'"

I raise an eyebrow. "The French have a definite way with words."

"Meanwhile, Chrétien's beside himself."

"Yeah," I say. "Kind of picked up on that."

"Apparently, when she died, Chrétien was going to burn his wife's diary, but Sir Walter convinced him that there might come a time he would want to read it. I guess she wrote a few entries toward the last days of her life that Chrétien couldn't bring himself to look at back then."

"Oh, wow. Bummer." Then I remember something. "Chrétien was reading a very old book just before he and I went clothes shopping together. He set it down to help me when my jeans button popped off. It had a brown leather cover."

"That was it," says Sam. "In our hurry to leave, he forgot all about it. Brown leather book, brown leather chair ... no one saw it."

"Fritz saw it," I say, angry. And then a small part of me does this little hop-skip-jump inside. Chrétien set down his wife's journal to go shopping with *me*. I don't want to read too much into that, obviously, but the symbolism is, as my English teacher would say, readily apparent for anyone who's awake.

"Maybe it's for the best," I say, slowly. "Maybe it will help Chrétien to let go of the past. Isn't that what he needs?"

Sam looks at me, her brows drawn together. "What Chrétien needs is his wife's diary back. You saw the look on his face just now."

I frown. I'm not sure Sam's right about this, based on things I've heard Ma say. "Let me ask you a question. Have you ever seen a picture of my dad at my place?"

"No," replies Sam.

"That's right," I say. "And you never will, either. My mom says the best thing she ever did to help her move on was to get rid of every trace of him. Trust me, this may hurt now, but it will help Chrétien in the long run."

Sam is quiet for a second, but then she shakes her head. "You can't compare the two things at all. They're completely different."

I raise an eyebrow. "They look pretty same-same to me."

Sam continues. "In the case of your mom, it was her choice. *Bridget's* choice." She wraps her hands around her arms in a sort of self-hug and looks at the fire. "There's a difference between choosing to let go of your past and having your past ripped out of your hands," she says quietly.

How do I respond to that? I mean, she's right,

obviously. There's a difference. But is it an important one?

I sigh. "Maybe you're right about choosing versus not choosing. I don't know." I don't say out loud the other stuff I'm thinking: that either way, after three hundred years, it is maybe time for Chrétien to think about moving on.

"Me neither," says Sam. "Not really. All I know is we can't let any offspring of Helmann's get that password."

A disturbing thought occurs to me. "Fritz's office is in San Francisco, right?" I ask. "Do you think Chrétien decided just now to zip back to San Francisco and steal the diary back?"

"Before you woke up, Will already suggested going to San Francisco, and Chrétien rejected the idea as too dangerous," says Sam. "They have rippler detection in the lab where Fritz works."

"Excuse me? How do you detect invisible, insubstantial people?"

"By temperature," says Sam. "If a rippler strolls into the lab, the change in temperature registers and they set it up to make the lights dim and a warning siren go off."

"Oh," I say. "That's handy. For them, I mean."

And for me, too. The more I think about it, the more I am glad Chrétien has had his hand forced, as it were. If he can say goodbye to his past, he's got a better chance at happiness now.

I look around the farmhouse. It's awfully quiet

with just me and Sam. A chill runs along my shoulders. How would I know if it wasn't just us?

"Why don't we have one of those temperature things?" I ask, looking around for signs of invisible kidnappers.

"We have Sir Walter," says Sam. "He hears what he calls people's 'thought signatures' when they are invisible and nearby."

"Oh. Right." Like me with Chrétien. I try listening for him for a sec, but he must not be talking to God at the moment. Or to me.

"By the way, I've been meaning to tell you something," I say. "Chrétien and I can converse when we're invisible. We found out on the car ride down here."

Sam's left brow arches. "You can *hear* him?"

I nod.

"I can't get Will to hear me," she says, sadly. "We have to send images. Sir Walter said it might get better someday, but so far it hasn't. Well, except now when we ripple, we can 'write' each other even if we're not touching." She sighs. "You're lucky."

I'm on the verge of saying something *very* sarcastic, but at the last minute, I don't.

Proof Gwyns can be reformed.

"It must be Chrétien," says Sam. "Sir Walter says he is exceptionally talented in that regard. Sort of a human amplifier."

"Chrétien's exceptional in a lot of regards, most of which are hidden under way too many layers of clothing," I murmur.

Proof Gwyns can't be reformed.

"Gwyn, we talked about this. No breaking his heart."

"Can't break what you can't touch." I'm light and breezy about it. Like it's not breaking *my* heart.

Sam looks worried still.

I take one of her hands in mine. "I know, Sam. I'm giving him a wide berth. I mean, wide for me."

She hugs me. "I just hate to see him suffering like this," she whispers.

Me, too. And for once, I don't try to make a joke out of it.

Chapter Eleven

MOVIE POPCORN NIGHT

Chrétien returns two hours later, arriving just after Sir Walter has come back and conjured a meal out of thin air. (Okay, a few cans and jars and wheels of cheese were maybe involved.) We are just sitting down together for a late lunch.

I pat the seat next to me. "Give me some sugar, sugar," I say to Chrétien. It's something I said all the time back home. It's flirty, I know, but for once I'm not trying to ... you know, *flirt*. I'm just hoping to redirect his thoughts to Las Abuelitas and to his life now. I wish I could stop that look of hurt on his face. This much of what I want for Chrétien is real and true and solid.

We talk about stuff over dinner, the five of us, but Chrétien doesn't exactly join in, beyond answering yes

106

and no a few times. I can't seem to do anything to cheer him up, although if I don't do something, I'm going to plunge right down the rabbit hole after him, I swear.

The whole room is catching Chrétien's sad mood, as if depression is contagious. Sir Walter gets quiet, and then Sam gets worried looking at Sir Walter being quiet, and then Will gets concerned about Sam looking worried. I mean, this cannot be allowed to continue. So I make a decision: the buck stops here.

"Okay," I say. "That's it. Movie Popcorn Night. Where's the computer?"

Everyone in the room stares at me.

"What?" I demand. "Why are you looking at me? Like that?"

Sam responds. "Movie … popcorn … night?"

"Yes," I say, crossing my arms. "It is totally a thing."

Will frowns. "I don't think they're big on popcorn in France."

"Fine," I say. "Movie pâté night then." I hold up a ceramic pot of pâté. "Or movie pickled onions night." I point to the jar of pickled onions.

"I take it 'movie popcorn night' is where you watch a movie and eat popcorn?" Sam asks.

"It's a Li family tradition," I say. "Because, you know, Ma's thing with cooking dinners. Or, rather, her thing with *not* cooking dinners."

"She makes dinners.," says Sam. "Just … weird ones."

107

"Organic popcorn is very healthy," says Will.

"Yup," I say. It's not like it ever bugged me eating popcorn or bakery leftovers. "Anyway, no biggie if we can't find popcorn. I'm sure popcorn has nothing on pâté and onions. So let's find a movie."

"Um...." says Sam, looking around the cottage.

"Mick's computer has internet," says Will. "I'm sure we can find something."

Ten minutes later, we are arguing over the selections on a French site devoted to *films américains*. I put the kibosh on *Romeo and Juliet*, both the Zeffirelli and the Leonardo DiCaprio versions, as suggested by Will. Sam, her eye on Chrétien, won't say yes to anything that's a straight comedy. It's looking like we'll never get Movie Popcorn Night started. But then I find one.

"Oh," I say, a bit of a sigh in my voice. "*Ever After* is perfect!"

No one but me has seen it, although I spend a minute trying to convince Sam and Will they *must* have seen it. But they're both pretty sure they haven't.

"It's okay you haven't seen it," I say. "That's perfect, actually. You will all love it. It's set in France. Long ago France, so there's something for Sir Walter, and it's a love story, so there's something for Sam, there's Leonardo da Vinci for Will, and Chrétien—you are just going to have to take my word for it: best Cinderella story *ever*."

As I say this, I remember Sam's weird warning when I wanted to do a paper on Cinderella. She's looking at Chrétien. I look over, too.

Chrétien manages a small smile, his mouth pulling up on one side. "Let us enjoy the performance," he says.

Sir Walter crosses to stoke the fire one last time, and then, with the computer set up on a low table, we snuggle onto the couch and against the couch, all five of us. It is very crowded, but no one minds.

The music starts and, for the next exactly one hundred minutes, I am swept up in this alternate world where fathers love their daughters, and hard work and attitude pay off, and it is just, *maybe*, possible to believe that an *ever after* might end happily.

The fire has died down, and when I glance up to Sir Walter, our usually enthusiastic stoker-of-fires, I see him wiping a tear from his face.

Will starts rattling off historical inaccuracies as the credits roll. "I mean, yes, Francis the First was patron to da Vinci," he begins. "But if you take into consideration—ow!" he says. "Broken leg, here!"

Sam glares at him. "That's why I punched your arm and not your leg," she says.

I smirk just a little because honestly, the way those two never disagree about anything can get a bit nauseating. Plus, how dare he attack the best Cinderella re-tell ever?

Chrétien rises from the couch. "I shall retire," he says quietly. "Thank you for the evening's entertainment," he says, turning to me. "It was most … *informative*."

Visible

I frown at Chrétien's broad back as he disappears (literally) for the night. *Informative?* What does that even mean?

"You must forgive my son," says Sir Walter. He strokes his goatee in his *"I'm worried"* way. "He is most distressed at the loss of his wife's diary."

"Do you think the movie made it worse?" I ask.

"I believe your kind intention in providing a distraction from the diary made it *better*," replies Sir Walter, solemnly.

"Can I ask you a question?" I ask. "What is it with all the journals and diaries anyway? I don't know one single person who does that in this century."

Sir Walter chuckles. "It is no longer the fashion; that is true enough. But consider for a moment your own devotion to the ... how do you call it?" He raises and contemplates his cell phone. "Ah, yes: the *social media*. Do you not therein record the manner in which your days are passed, whether by word or by picture?"

"Huh," I say. "I guess, when you put it that way, my generation *does* journal. We just do it more publicly."

Sir Walter does one of his little nods that means, *yes.*

I swear I should write a book on French gestural language. For a nation that loves its mother tongue, they sure say a lot without words.

The fire is pretty much dead now, and we all sit without talking for several minutes. I get up, finally, and tell everyone good night. The bed is cold, but the down-filled blanket is warm. My last thoughts are about ballet and the language of gesture and whether the French say stuff with their bodies because of Louis Quatorze's obsession with dance.

When I wake up, it's dark, although there's a stripe of moonlight streaking through the window. I can't figure why I am awake when the sun isn't up, and I'm feeling pretty grumpy about it, frankly, because I was dreaming I was Danielle de Barbarac and Chrétien was Prince Henry, which is a much nicer thing to be focusing on in the middle of the night than Will's noisy sleep breathing in the main room.

For a minute, I figure that is what woke me up. Will isn't snoring exactly, but he's a pretty noisy breather. But then I realize it's singing that woke me up. A particular kind of singing. The kind made by a seventeenth century Catholic who's been transported into the twenty-first century with his old habits intact.

"Chrétien," I mumble to myself.

Ugh. Now that I can hear him chanting, there is no way I'm falling asleep until I tell him to knock it off already. I'm pretty sure God is fine with you chanting prayers in your mind without … *intending* the words to fly "out there" or whatever.

I stumble out of bed, trying to remember where it was that Chrétien was supposed to sleep. Out in the main room, Will has the couch. Sam's got the other room in the house. What's left? And then I remember Sir Walter was going to ripple instead of taking up a bed. I saw Chrétien ripple last night, too, so he must

111

be doing the same thing.

Except that I can hear him. He's got to be around here somewhere.

"Chrétien?" I whisper so I don't wake anyone up. He must be solid somewhere close based on how loud and clear he's singing right now. I look in the bathroom because I made him hang out in my bath to sing prayers a couple weeks ago when he brought Sam back from being kidnapped and having an egg harvested. Remembering Sam's ordeal, I shudder. At least I was only kidnapped and drugged.

He's not in the bathroom, however. That leaves Sam's room and the kitchen. Although, if Chrétien is chanting in Latin over my sleeping best friend, that would just weird me out beyond belief. I have caught him glancing at her with this wistful, sad expression.

Oh, no.

Does Chrétien have feelings for Sam?

If there is anything sadder than Chrétien not falling head over heels in love with Yours Truly, it would be Chrétien falling in love with Already Taken. I swing back to Sam's room, but he's not there. Thankfully.

He's not in the kitchen, either. Although without any moonlight on this side of the house, I could be missing him if he were sitting really still.

"Chrétien?" I call out into the darkened room.

He's not here. I turn back to the main room just in time to see him ripple solid in front of the fireplace.

"*Holy guacamole and salsa!*" I hiss-whisper.

Will, on the couch, doesn't even twitch. Mick said something about how he could sleep through a convoy of ambulances, sirens blaring.

"*Mademoiselle?*" Chrétien whispers back.

"Shh!" I bring one finger to my lips and point to Will with the other.

He walks very close to me. So close I can feel his breath on my neck as he whispers in my ear. "You require my presence?"

I grab his hand and march him into the kitchen so we can talk. Chrétien's hand in mine feels warm, and I curse myself for not shoving him by the shoulders instead because now I'll just have to let go of his hand again, and I *so* don't want to let go.

But I get us to the long table where we all ate dinner and let his hand slip from mine and let out a long exasperated sigh. For oh, so many reasons.

"You were chanting your prayers and it woke me up. I thought you were in my room or next door or something."

"*Mademoiselle*," he says, "I beg your pardon. I was in my chameleon form. I did not think to be overheard."

"You were invisible?"

From somewhere on the table, Chrétien finds and strikes a match. He lights one of the large candles on the table. His face is furrowed in concentration as he tries to light a second candle before the match burns his fingers. He doesn't quite make it and winces, then brings his finger to his mouth.

Oh, dear God. Those fingers. That mouth. I look away. I swallow hard and try to remember why I am here.

Chrétien tilts his head to one side and answers my question from a minute ago. "I was, indeed, invisible when I was chanting the hours. And yet, you report that you could hear me?"

I nod. In the flicker of the candles' light, Chrétien's face is all angles and planes. His eyes are darker, too. He is altogether the most perfect thing I have ever laid eyes on. And he's altogether unavailable. I look away.

"I suppose," he says, "that in addressing God Most High, I may be considered as intending my voice to reach outward. It would make sense that you heard, in that case."

"Yeah, but you were invisible and I was solid. Doesn't that make it weird that I heard you?"

Chrétien shrugs. The light dances, golden, across his face. "We have … what is the word? *Connected*. You have become attuned to my thoughts, perhaps."

Connected. Great. Because that is so what I need right now. I sigh.

Chrétien frowns. "I wonder that *Mademoiselle* Samantha never heard me."

Oh, I do know about this. "She heard you, Chrétien. She told me it kept her up nights, too. She also said something about the Catholic Church no longer requiring the same, um, prayer schedule. So you might want to check up on that."

He does a head-bow-acquiescence thing.

"I shall ask my father. And tonight, I shall chant no more. Forgive, if you please, my unintentional disturbing of your rest."

"That's okay," I say. "You looked like … you looked like you could use some, uh, divine solace tonight." I seriously don't know where the word "solace" came from. I don't recall its being a part of the Gwyn vocab. Must be a Chrétien word.

Chrétien tries to smile, but it only makes him look more miserable than ever.

My heart pinches. "That's why I thought of doing a movie," I say softly. "You know, to take your mind off things. Like when I was worried in the car about falling through the road and you told me a story to distract me."

I'm rewarded with another of his almost-smiles. He looks down at his hands, resting on the table. His lashes look a mile long with the shadows cast by the flickering candlelight.

"The movie was a welcome distraction," he says. And then I hear him silently add, *But….*

"I heard that," I say. "It was distracting but *what?*"

Chrétien's smile is whole this time. "It was a fiction. A *tissu* … that is, a *fabric* of inaccuracies."

"Um, yeah. It was a fairytale. I don't think they're supposed to be big on 'accurate.'"

And in my head, I hear Chrétien ask me a question.

Would you like to hear the true story of the little cinder

115

girl?

"There's a true version?"

But of course.

Chrétien is quite comfortable with the whole mind meld thing, but I have to say it is weirding me out a bit. "Sure," I say out loud. "I love a good story."

By which I mean, "*I love your voice.*"

Let us go out of doors, Chrétien says. *So we do not wake the others.*

"Um, February? Cold. Very cold, Chrétien. This sweater is all I have." I pinch at one of my shoulders to show it's not exactly a thick woolly number.

We could ripple. You will feel not the cold. Will you allow me to take once more your hand? he asks.

I just about choke on my own spit when he asks, but I nod, too. And then for a moment, Chrétien's hand is in mine, and I feel his pulse against mine where our wrists touch, and I smell something— cardamom? Allspice?—and then we are invisible.

We pass through the ancient stone of the cottage wall and out into a flood of moonlight where Chrétien tells me a story.

Chapter Twelve

LA CENDRILLON

Once upon a time, in England, there lived a mother who was delivered of a beautiful girl after a barren marriage of ten years. The daughter was the joy and solace of her parents, who sang and danced for the pleasure of the king and queen. The birth of the daughter lent new strength to her parents, seeming, as it were, to make them young once more, which they neither of them had been for many years. The mother's gray hairs turned back to gold and the father's once-sparse hair grew now lustily upon his head, and the father and mother danced before the king and queen more beautifully than ever before.

The king and queen were very pleased with the players and invited them often to court where they were presented with gifts of rich cloth, sometimes embroidered with silver or golden thread.

But more precious to the father and mother than threads of

gold was the flowing mane of gold and copper upon the head of their beloved daughter, Maria Anna. When Maria Anna was old enough to walk, she learned to dance. When she was old enough to babble, she learned to sing. And so sweetly did she sing that she made courtiers who had been enemies with one another embrace in forgiveness and brotherhood. The queen was so enchanted with the copper-haired girl that she presented Maria Anna's mother with a length of cloth-of-silver.

I interrupt Chrétien. *Wait a minute*, I say. *I thought you said women weren't allowed on the stage.*

Chrétien replies. *Indeed,* Mademoiselle, *they were not permitted upon the public stage. However, in private performances, it was sometimes permissible for a female to perform.*

Okay, I say. *Carry on.*

Chrétien laughs softly.

The queen was so enchanted with the copper-haired girl that she presented Maria Anna's mother with a length of cloth-of-silver.

"When your child has grown to her full size, you must make for her a pair of silver slippers. For never have I seen a more lively or more natural dancer. But wait until her feet attain their full size, for otherwise you will regret cutting into the cloth of silver."

Maria Anna's mother bowed low to the queen and promised to do as she said.

Later that year, the plague broke out in London, and the theatres were closed, and the king and queen requested no private plays, "Lest we should appear to make merry whilst our people suffer and die," said the king.

But by the time the danger of plague had passed, the courtiers who had formerly been enchanted by the girl Maria Anna had become once more bitter enemies and many of them said to one another, "Let us close the playhouses, which breed sinners and all manner of evil." And so the playhouses were closed, and Maria Anna's father and mother and all her many cousins had to find a new way to earn the bread they ate and the wine they drank.

And the day came when Maria Anna's father had spent the last of the coin set aside for times when players could not find employment, and he said to his wife, "Shall we go hungry indeed whilst we have yet the length of cloth of silver from her majesty the queen?"

But Maria Anna's mother declared that she would sooner die than sell the cloth of silver meant to adorn the feet of their lovely daughter when, one day, Maria Anna should reach her full grown stature. And Maria Anna's mother was as good as her word, too, perishing from hunger not three weeks later.

Some fathers might, perhaps, have sold the cloth of silver in a fit of anger and despair. But Maria Anna's father said he had not the heart to sell that which had not brought unto his wife health while she yet lived. By now, Maria Anna's cousins and aunties and uncles had all fled England which had become a place of war, and which, moreover, was a place where players were no longer safe, for even the king himself had been executed by the warmongering courtiers.

And so Maria Anna and her father braved the wild sea to journey to France where her father hoped he could find a castle or inn in need of such entertainment as he and his daughter could provide. They traveled through the countryside, but they found no lasting employment. Sometimes a farmer or farmwife would give the lovely child and her poor father a gift of eggs or of milk or of bread, but no one wanted a song or a play in the countryside.

At last they came to Paris, the great city, where they fell in among a company of poor players who were nonetheless generous of heart. They sang and danced in the streets of Paris, and though their bellies were often empty, their hearts were full.

One day, it happened that a woman among the players who had lost her beauty to the pox cast her eyes upon Maria Anna's father, promising with those eyes pleasures the father had sorely missed since the death of his dear wife. And so, presently, Maria Anna's father married the French woman, and Maria Anna gained also a pair of sisters. Thanks to the step-mother's connections, the family of five traveled to court on Christmas day to sing for the French king and queen.

"Only you must now be called Marie-Anne, which is a proper name in France," said the copper-haired girl's new mother.

Marie-Anne nodded and sang and danced for the king and the queen who declared themselves enchanted by the little golden angel. But this made Marie-Anne's new mother jealous for the chances of her own dear daughters to charm the court, and so Marie-Anne was set to brushing clean the costumes and beating the rugs upon which the family slept by night. And she was left to sleep by the fire at night, for, as her stepmother said, there was no room for a child in the bed of a husband and wife, and the sisters had only a small carpet between them as well.

Marie Anne did not complain, and besides, she liked watching the bright embers as she drifted each night to sleep. If she was sooty come morning, well, at least she had kept warm beside the dying fire.

In due time, Marie-Anne's dear father became ill and, having lain down, did not rise again. Marie-Anne begged of her father that he allow her to sell her cloth of silver to buy medicine for him, but he would not permit her to do this.

"When you are grown, see a cobbler and have him make for you a pair of silver slippers," said her father. And he breathed his last and died.

When once Marie-Anne's father had left this world for a better one, the true nature of Marie-Anne's belle-mère, *her step-mother, became apparent. Her belle-mère made of Marie-Anne a sort of slave whose job it was to do all the most distasteful tasks. As, the washing of small clothes, the sweeping from the chimney of soot, and the emptying of the chamber pots.*

But Marie-Anne did not complain. In truth, she had no heart for dancing now that her dear mother and her dear father had gone to live with the holy angels. And so she cleaned and swept and scrubbed and sang only to please herself.

One day, it happened that the cruel belle-mère discovered the length of cloth of silver given Marie-Anne by the queen of England.

"Why, you wretched child," shouted the belle- mère. "Shall you have cloth of silver while your sisters wear thrice-turned coats?"

And in spite of Marie-Anne's great distress, her step-mother took from her the cloth of silver and traveled to court where she thought to sell it for a great sum. But when the wicked belle-mère came to court, she was accused of having thieved the length of cloth of silver and she was hung on the spot for her theft.

121

News of the loss of her step-mother reached Marie-Anne only after the passage of several days. Her step-sisters wept and Marie-Anne wept, too, for she was tender of heart, although the step-mother had proven herself no friend to Marie-Anne.

But after a week of tears, Marie-Anne declared that they three girls must find a way to keep themselves from hunger or prostitution, and Marie-Anne determined to visit the court of the queen and the dauphin, who was now heir-apparent following the king's death, but too young to rule. Having heard that the young dauphin had inherited his mother's love of theatricals, Marie-Anne was in high hopes of finding employment for herself and her sisters with such acting or dancing troupes as might lodge near the royal court.

Moreover, all three were comely of appearance, which the French valued in their players even more than did the English. Marie-Anne made herself acquainted with a troupe of dancers who performed for the queen and her royal son. And while it was not permitted for a woman to dance in France, the lead danseur of the troupe took pity on the copper-haired English girl.

Marie-Anne then was engaged along with her sisters to do the washing and carry the ashes for the troupe of dancers in royal residence at the queen's château. But after a month, her two sisters took lovers saying they had no wish to work as laborers when they might earn their bread and wine more easily upon their backs.

Marie-Anne was saddened at the loss of her sisters, but she threw herself all the more into the service of the troupe. And in time, she learned the French style of dancing and singing and acting. And gradually, she was no longer required to carry away the ashes or to launder the clothing but was employed as *seamstress, often laboring alongside the troupe as they rehearsed for the better fitting and altering of their garments.*

And in time, when there was any question as to the manner in which one ballet or another was to be performed, they consulted Marie-Anne, for having once seen it, she could remember anything at all.

"Oh, we cannot do without Marie-Anne," said the singing master and the dancing master.

And then, one day, when the young man who played the parts of the shepherdesses and young wenches fell ill from too much wine, the dancing master told Marie-Anne that she must dance his roles instead, for they were ordered to perform for her majesty the queen and his majesty the dauphin.

Thus, when she was fourteen, Marie-Anne was presented yet again before a queen. And the French queen declared herself so enchanted with the copper-haired "boy" that she presented the twice-disguised Marie-Anne with a pair of her own royal shoes, with diamond buckles and made from cloth of gold.

And Marie-Anne, who had once lived among the sooty ashes of the hearth, now lived at court, dancing and singing for the queen and the dauphin for many pleasant years.

~ ~ ~

That's the end of the story? I ask, when Chrétien falls silent.

He doesn't respond.

Chrétien?

Forgive me, Mademoiselle, *do you not hear the voice of my father?*

I listen, but I hear nothing. Or maybe I do hear a tiny something. *Do you hear him?*

Indeed, Mademoiselle. *He is calling for me. Let us repair unto the house.*

Which I'm guessing is antiquated English for "go inside."

Chrétien, I say. *Was that really the end of the story?*

Stories, Mademoiselle, *have many endings. That was one.*

I want to tell Chrétien that was the lamest re-tell of *La Cendrillon* in the history of the world. Where's the ball? Where's the pumpkin? Where's the marriage to the prince?

If that is the true story of the cinder girl, then I will eat my running shoes.

Chrétien carries us across the pavement and back to the cottage where he speaks to me again. *I must bring us into our solid forms in order to release you.*

You got it, I reply.

We shiver invisibly through the door before Chrétien brings us back solid again inside the main room of the farmhouse. Will's up now. And Sam. The fire crackles and pops.

Sir Walter speaks softly to Chrétien.

And I catch the word *dangereuse.*

Chapter Thirteen

QUEEN OF GOOD CHEER

"Fritz sent another video," says Will, as soon as he sees me and Chrétien. He cues it up for us to watch.

In this latest, Fritz reminds us of the deadline (now less than thirty hours) and tells us of his *disappointment that he has not heard back from Sir Walter.*

Lacking anything better to do, Fritz continues, *I decided to read my lady's diary. Perhaps it ought to be preserved after all. We have here everyday descriptions of the queen of France, juicy snippets of gossip, sketches of a sweet child—perhaps the one who falls ill? Where is that entry ...*

Fritz flips to the back of the diary.

Ah, yes. Here it is.

He reads from the diary, translating it into English as he goes.

"The dowager queen paid me this day a visit unexpected, leaving a bottle of wine of her decoction for my darling child. And in truth Madeleine is most unwell."

Fritz looks up at us from the computer.

But how is it this did not strike me earlier? The world should see this. What a perfect window into everyday life in the time of the Sun King. There is some ongoing controversy concerning the queen, is there not? What do you think, cousin? Shall I share your son's secrets with the world at large? Or shall we make an exchange: my father's secrets for your son's?

Chrétien's face is white as death. He must have been holding his breath as well, because it all comes out in a whoosh—the sound of a man pushed to his limits.

He storms to the door, vanishing into invisibility just before he reaches it.

"Shouldn't someone … go after him?" I ask. And for once I'm not thinking about me being the someone. "You're his father," I say to Sir Walter. "Go talk to him."

But Sir Walter shakes his head. "He does not ask it of me."

"Oh, good grief!" I say. I run to the front door and throw it open. There's no sign of Chrétien. Just a cold, dark morning.

I sigh heavily. I can no more find him than I could find a particular drop of water in a river. He's gone. Returning inside, I close the door.

"Perhaps I should have better warned him," says Sir Walter.

But I don't think it would have helped. There are things you can't prepare for ahead of time.

"There must be laws about this," I say. "If Fritz delivers the contents to a film crew or university or whoever, Chrétien could come forward and say it's his wife's private journal."

"There's the problem of Chrétien's age," says Will, glum. "And how long ago his wife, the diarist, died."

"Oh, right," I say. So, no legal recourse.

Sam walks over to me, holding out a bowl-sized mug of café au lait.

"Good morning, sunshine," she says to me.

I raise one eyebrow. "You're mocking me."

"You look like you didn't sleep very well."

I grunt out a small laugh. "Chrétien was chanting in the middle of the night. It woke me up."

"I've learned to filter it out," Sam says, taking a sip from her own bowl of coffee.

"We talked for a long time," I tell her. "And he told me the weirdest version of the Cinderella story, like, ever."

"Oh, dear," says Sam. "He told you? He must be obsessing about everything. Isn't it the saddest story?"

Sad? It ended abruptly, but not sadly. I wonder if he didn't tell me the same story he told Sam. I'm prevented from asking Sam any questions by Chrétien rippling solid next to the door.

He bows to us. "You will please forgive my lack of self-control," he says. "Of course we must refuse this latest offer of the son of Helmann."

I frown, trying to figure out if he's really over his earlier outburst of emotion. He looked pretty upset when he heard Fritz wanted to broadcast his wife's diary to the world at large. But now he looks calm. Although, it's pretty hard to argue for trading back Helmann's journal for Chrétien's wife's diary.

I think back to the argument I made yesterday with Sam—how Chrétien would only really recover if he let go of his past. Well, maybe this is him on the road to recovery, finally.

The morning wears on with Sam and Will snuggling on the couch and me trying to write the French class paper. Chrétien offers answers to my questions about some of the finer points of ballet in the court of King Louis the Fourteenth. But in the hour following lunch, Chrétien does a lot of pacing and sighing. I decide this will not do. Not at all. I'm just not sure how to fix it.

At last, Chrétien announces that he will, perhaps, take a walk outside.

More time alone to brood? That is *not* what he needs. And with a flash of clarity like when you solve a math problem, I realize how I can help. Operation Catch Chrétien is officially terminated. (There wasn't much hope there, anyway.) And Operation Cheer Chrétien Up is officially launching.

Now that I think of it, it sort of launched last night with the movie. This is the kind of thing I am good at. Being the life of the party. Cheering people up. That's it! No more Queen of Messing Up Relationships. From here on, I am the Queen of Good Cheer.

I nudge Sam. "Let's see if he wants company," I say. "A distraction. We could go into town. I need croissants and more clothes."

Sam nods and we ask Chrétien if he would mind company.

"But of course I would not mind," he says, bowing slightly.

We hike up to Carcassonne, which is a pretty kickin' medieval town, all spires and cobblestones, enclosed by impressive walls. It's a warm afternoon, and we are all enchanted by the way the sun hits the turrets and sparkles off leaded glass windows.

Operation Cheer Chrétien Up is working well, if I'm any judge.

After several purchases and several visits to *patisseries,* I'm just starting to think we should be getting back because the shops are closing and I'm finally tired. That would be my essay on this trip if I had to write one: "How I Went to France and Got Really Tired."

Beside me, Chrétien and Sam are talking about rippling and 'thought signatures' and I don't know what all else. I just walk alongside them, occasionally letting the two of them go in front of me if it gets crowded or narrow. There are, after all, considerable compensations for walking behind Chrétien.

We get outside the town walls, and Sam notices

the sun's going down.

"It's going to be in the eyes of any motorists driving home," she says.

"Shall we assume our chameleon forms?" asks Chrétien.

"Hello," I say from behind. "Visible girl. Still here."

"But of course, *Mademoiselle*," says Chrétien. "I would be honored to transport you."

"Beam me up, Scotty," I say.

"I beg your pardon?" Chrétien looks puzzled.

"He's never watched the SyFy channel, obviously," I say to Sam. Then, speaking to Chrétien, I hold my hand out and say, "I'm all yours."

This time I catch the heady scent of almond from some pastry we ate earlier that I couldn't pronounce alongside the spice I can't name. Cloves? Cinnamon? And then we're invisible and we *tear* down the road. I remember Ma saying how Chrétien got her from our Midpines cabin to Las Abs faster than a car could have driven it, and now I get why she said she never wanted to ripple again. I mean, *I* don't feel that way, but Ma drives like a little old grandma to save gas. She *hates* when I drive fast. And this is way, way faster than we could go in a car.

I love it.

Far too soon, we're back to the cottage, and we come solid out front, me feeling breathless and exhilarated and realizing I didn't say a single word to Chrétien the whole time. I give his hand a quick squeeze.

"That was super fun!" I whisper.

He smiles and slips from my grasp, in a way that reflects real life pretty darned accurately.

Inside, Sir Walter's cute little cottage looks a bit dumpy after the slate-roofed turrets of Carcassonne. But the fire is warm, and Sir Walter's cassoulet for dinner is delicious, and soon I'm feeling drowsy again.

"Gwyn. Wake up," says Sam.

I twitch. Open my eyes. I've fallen asleep on the couch. "Ripple me back to my bed?"

Sam snorts at the idea. But then she takes my hand, ripples us both invisible, and pops me in my snug bed. I could get used to having someone like this always at my beck and call. I'm asleep pretty much instantly.

Some time later, I wake up in pitch darkness. I heard someone shouting. A name. *Marie-Anne!* I can almost hear the echo fade from the room. I sit up, listening. It takes me a minute to place where I've heard that name before, but then I remember I heard it last night during *Story Hour: The Lame Retelling of Cinderella.* I blink my eyes. I'm thirsty as anything. Cassoulet is delicious, but Sir Walter sure didn't skimp on the salt.

I wander in the dark to the kitchen, stubbing my toe once on the corner of the wall and once on the table leg. I keep the swearing in my head, just barely, although that second time nearly does me in.

"Hello," says Chrétien. His sudden appearance

accomplishes what the toe-stubs couldn't: he scares the swear words right out of me.

"Did I startle you?" he asks.

"Um, let me think a sec … *YES!*" The "s" sound comes out as a hiss because I'm whispering. "Of course, that would be *in addition* to the part where you woke me up."

"I awakened you, *Mademoiselle?*"

"Yeah," I say, fumbling for a cup in the dark. "Talking to yourself, I presume. I'll thank you to keep the bed times stories *un*-intended for public dissemination, if you don't mind."

"Bed time stories?"

"That lame version of the Cinderella story," I say. "Where she's called Marie-Anne. I heard you speak that name and it woke me up."

Chrétien doesn't say anything. Not even, *I beg pardon, Mademoiselle.*

"Never mind," I say. "I need a drink of water. If you'll excuse me." As I'm chugging down the water, I start feeling bad. I mean, Chrétien's already had a sucky day. Time to reengage the Cheer Chrétien Up protocol.

"Hey," I say. "I'm sorry for my bad manners. I'm sorry about your day, too. And about Fritz. And I apologize for calling your story lame. It's just different from the story I grew up with."

Chrétien lights a candle like he did last night.

"We've got to stop meeting like this," I say.

"Must we? Wherefore?"

132

He actually wants to know why we can't. Meet. Like this.

"It was a joke. Ignore it." I finish the water in my cup. "I'm always trying to be funny. Sometimes it's not the right time for funny."

I look up and see those candle-illuminated cheekbones. So sharp they could give you a paper-cut.

"It was a long time ago," says Chrétien.

I'm guessing we're back to talking about his version of Cinderella.

"I am told," he continues, "that my friend *Monsieur* Perrault wrote the tale down in a fashion that has endured. Perhaps that is the tale with which *Mademoiselle* is familiar. With the *fée marraine* and the white mice and the slipper of glass?"

"Yeah," I say. "Fairy godmother. Mice. Glass footwear. Although, the whole glass shoe thing always bugged me. I mean, talk about uncomfortable. I'll take those cloth of gold slippers any day over glass."

Chrétien smiles, and I feel all warm and snuggly, like that moment when you grab a bunch of fluffy towels straight from the dryer. I smile back.

"Marie-Anne would have liked your version of her story," says Chrétien. "The movie with da Vinci."

"Oh, would she now? And what makes you so sure?"

Chrétien's eyes draw together. Puzzled. "We were married ... intimate, you know. I just know she would prefer your version over Perrault's white mice."

My mouth forms a tiny *o* of understanding: *Marie-*

Anne was the wife he lost. He said her name into the dark night because he's, you know, missing her and miserable without her and doesn't even have her diary to console him anymore.

"Oh, Chrétien, I am so sorry," I say, the words rushing together in one multi-syllabic mess.

"In what way do you believe you have occasioned offense?"

I shake my head. "How many ways are there?" I take my head in my hands. "I didn't know that was your wife. In the story. I thought it was something you just … you know, made up. I didn't know that story … *mattered* to you, on a personal level."

"You have not offended me in your manner of speech about Marie-Anne," says Chrétien. "And you are correct in that, while it is the time of sleeping, I ought to keep in better restraint those thoughts I have of her. Or upon any subject. I apologize for waking you."

"It's fine," I say. "My internal clock is stuck on California time, I think."

"I have difficulty sleeping as well," says Chrétien, sighing.

We smile sadly at each other and then both look away. I watch the shadows cast on the far wall by the flickering candle.

Chrétien speaks. "While it is most considerate of you to pass the time entertaining me, I must insist you return to your rest."

"Entertaining you?" I guffaw. "Right. Because I'm

totally as fun as YouTube kitten videos. Said no one. Ever."

Chrétien looks at me, amused.

Well, I live for the laugh. Although, I wonder what life would look like if I didn't?

"Shall I escort you to your sleeping chamber?" he asks.

I shake my head. "I'm wide awake."

"Perhaps, then, a stroll under the refulgence of the moon?"

"Dude, where do you get these words?"

Chrétien's brows draw together.

"Never mind. The answer's yes."

"You are not, I judge, clothed for a walk in solid form."

I look down. I'm in a tank and boy shorts. And I didn't think about this until just now? I am so losing my game.

But that's not it. Not really. It's strange, but when it comes right down to it, I don't want to play games with Chrétien. Not anymore. I'm not sure I know how to be friends with a guy—I don't have a lot of experience with "just friends," but I think, maybe, it might be nice to try it for once. And it definitely fits better in the Cheer Chrétien protocol I've adopted.

I smile and hold my hand out. "We'll be warm once we ripple."

Chrétien takes in my apparel again. His cheeks flush, which, in candlelight, just looks like darkening. He is all hard edges and lit planes.

I drop my hand. "You know what? Let me quick put on a sweater."

He averts his gaze, nodding.

I slip back to my room and grab my sweater. Then, for good measure, I pull on some leggings I bought in Carcassonne. Sneaking back down the hall, I shake my head. Who am I and what did I do with Gwyn?

Chapter Fourteen

THE GOLDEN SLIPPER

A few minutes later, Chrétien and I are strolling invisibly along the drive in front of his father's cottage. The moon is very ... *refulgent*, indeed. It looks bright enough to read by. Or close to it. I hear Chrétien humming. I don't recognize the tune, but it sounds lullabye-ish, almost. He breaks off abruptly.

You must miss them a ton, I say, inside our invisibly melded brains.

Yes, he replies, a response both simple and heartbreaking.

I feel his heaviness almost like it's my own. I want so much to make things better, but where would I even start?

Would it help to ... talk about them? I ask. I know I'm inviting him to visit the past, but it feels like the right thing to do, somehow.

Perhaps. My father is now of the opinion he did me no service, leaving me to my own thoughts through the centuries.

Through the centuries. I shudder. Well, my mind shudders. There's no Gwyn at the moment.

Was that super creepy? I ask. Being trapped all that time?

I was not trapped, Mademoiselle. *At any time, had I wished it, I could have regained motion and a physical form.*

So you didn't ... wish, I guess?

It was restful. More so than slumber, perhaps. Time seemed ... fluid ... unimportant. I do not know when I would have returned of my own volition, had not my father asked it of me when he did.

I try to think how to ask what I want to know. *Are you ... sorry you came back?*

No, he replies at once. *I am most glad to have rejoined my father. To have formed so many new acquaintance. To live once more among the visible.*

He says he's glad, but he seems sadder than ever. I'm about to say he can tell me whatever he wants, when he speaks again.

In truth, I do not know whether to desire to have Marie-Anne's diary once more or whether to be glad of its loss. Do you have the aphorism, 'to open once more a wound'?

Sure, I say. *Ma uses that phrase. Or one like it. She doesn't like when the aunties talk about the Chinese Cultural Revolution. She calls it "re-opening an old wound."*

Yes, says Chrétien. *Had our daughter lived, I should have liked to have kept my wife's diary, but perhaps it is better to allow the wounds to heal now.*

As he says this, I feel hope settle around us like a warm blanket. We stroll (or whatever this is) in silence for a few minutes, just enjoying the way the moonlight catches the tops of the trees, the roof, even Sir Walter's car.

Then Chrétien speaks again. *I have yet one other remembrance of Marie-Anne. I wonder, would you like to see the slipper of gold and diamond in which she danced with* le Roi-Soleil?

You have her shoes? I ask.

I have only one, he says. *I keep it hidden in the pocket of a jacket. The jacket rests invisibly within the wall of Château Rochefort.*

I hesitate. Does this fall in the category of reopening old wounds? Or the category of cheering Chrétien up? He seems eager to show me the golden slipper. And, seriously, is there any girl alive who doesn't want to see Cinderella's shoe? Maybe there is. But I'm not her.

I'd love to see it, I tell him. *Is Château Rochefort far?*

Chrétien laughs. *It is very close,* Mademoiselle. *Especially if you travel there with me.*

He picks up the pace like a jet taking off and we go from stroll to supersonic before he's done talking. A minute later, we're ascending a graveled side road. There are hardly any trees on the hill, so the castle catches my eye right away.

It's in ruins, I say. Completely unnecessarily. He's got to know this already.

I find it fair to behold, nevertheless, he says.

It's more than fair-to-behold. It's stunning. The moon lights up the stone to a nearly blinding white. The shadows are crisp, hard-edged like the angles of Chrétien's face.

Ohhhh, I sigh. *It's so* ... I don't know what the words are. I feel this ache where I know my chest should be and this longing. For what? I'm not sure. It's like I want to press into the castle, or like I want to fly into the sky to view it from above. Or maybe I want both at the same time. I want to run my fingers along every stone, listen for whispers of the people who built it, who lived here and died here.

I hear Chrétien's voice. *You are sad*, Mademoiselle?

How does he know this? *You can't see my face, can you?*

He sighs. *The heart sees what the eye cannot.*

I don't know how to respond to that. It's so ... personal.

How long has it been since anyone lived here? I ask at last.

I know not. My father tells me the castle changed hands many times following the revolution. I am glad I saw that not. Some things are sad enough within the pages of history, are they not?

Sad. That's part of how the ruined castle makes me feel. Sad to have not seen it in all its former glory. But it is so achingly beautiful now, with stones tumbling down like cascading water, and leaves growing through the arrow-slits along the walls.

Come, says Chrétien. *Let us find the slipper of La*

Cendrillon, *of the cinder girl.*

Sounds great, I say. Which is a stupid thing to say, really, when you're talking to the guy who married and lost Cinderella.

Chrétien, do you mind if I ask a question about your story?

I am at your service, he replies.

So, in the versions I know, the prince always marries the girl with the slipper. Isn't that kind of an important part of the story to change?

Ah, says Chrétien. *It is, indeed. I told you not the story in its entirety. Would you like to hear more?*

Sure, I say. *But not if it's going to make you sad. I mean, didn't you just say something about not opening old wounds?*

Chrétien's laughter, soft, fills my mind. *Mademoiselle is observant. But, perhaps I may find relief, even if I also find sorrow. But first, let us retrieve the slipper of gold.*

We pass through the castle wall, which I swear tickles, and then we start heading down a staircase. Which doesn't make a lot of sense unless castles have basements. This being France, I suppose it could be a wine cellar. I'm about to ask Chrétien where exactly his wife's shoe is hidden when we pass through a door and into a large room where the floor seems to waver.

I focus on the floor and realize it's *water.* There's an underground swimming pool here at Château Rochefort. Because, of course. Why wouldn't there be?

Wow, I say to Chrétien.

This place is called the Well of Juno, he tells me.

Oh. Yup. Sam told me about the Well. People died here. And started babies here. But, honestly, I can't find it in me to be creeped out by all those things because the place is so lovely. Coming through a hole in the roof, there's a shaft of moonlight—an *actual* shaft of moonlight—and it's suffusing the whole chamber with this silvery glow.

Chrétien has moved us close to a wall now, and it must be the wall where he hid his stuff, because he asks if I want to come solid to look at the slipper.

I peel my gaze from the water and say, *yes!*

A second later, I'm slipping my hand from Chrétien's. I expect it to be cold, but it's nice in this cave, or Well of Juno, or whatever. Chrétien is holding a satin robe-looking thing. He gives it a quick shake. It looks like something out of, I don't know, *Downton Abbey* or *Pride and Prejudice*, so basically, something Ma would love and no guy alive would be caught dead wearing today. Chrétien checks the pockets. The first one is empty, which makes him frown. Then he checks the second one and pulls out the world's smallest dancing shoe made of solid gold.

Okay, so obviously not solid gold, but now I get why the *cloth of silver* in the story was such a big deal. This must be made of ... cloth of *gold*, and it's breathtaking. The diamond buckle is beautiful, too. And huge, like the square kind of buckle you see on pilgrims' shoes. The diamonds catch a bit of moonlight and throw it back at the ceiling. I gaze up, my head shaking in wonder, and then I look back at the shoe.

"May I?" I ask, holding my hand outstretched.

"But, of course," says Chrétien.

It's heavier than I was expecting. I remember picking up a pair of ballet shoes once—the kind for dancing pointe—and being surprised how heavy they were for something that looks so dainty. It's the same with this shoe. I so want to try it on, but no way am I asking a grieving man if I can wear his dead wife's slipper, so I just run my fingers down the inside where it's covered in satin and hold it up to catch more moonlight.

"Seeing the slipper, I can just imagine her as she was," says Chrétien. He's got a tiny smile on his face. "Objects can do that, I suppose. Ground one ... tie one to what is no more."

Not what Dr. Gwyn would recommend, exactly. I say nothing.

Chrétien asks me if I am ready to hear more of the story of the cinder girl.

I look over and nod, *yes*.

"Shall we sit?" he asks, gesturing to the floor.

I settle with my back to the wall behind us and the pool of water before us and Cinderella's shoe in my hand. Chrétien begins.

"Once upon a time," he says, "in the days before prince Louis was crowned king, and while he yet lived in some fear of never becoming king, there was a loyal minister called Mazarin who advised him that he must

143

always, *always*, act the part of the king he hoped to become.

"And, to this end, his chief minister planned a grand *fête*, a great party, to which all the nobles of the land were commanded. And the chief part of the entertainment was to be a ballet of eight hours—"

"*Eight* hours?" I ask, interrupting the tale. "Are you sure you got that right? Eight like *huit* in French?"

Chrétien nods. "His majesty performed in ballets of twelve and thirteen hours upon other occasions."

I try to imagine a flash mob lasting for hours. It would be cool, but I honestly can't imagine who would have that kind of dedication.

Chrétien clears his throat and continues. "Within the ballet would be demonstrated the triumph of Reason over Ignorance, of Order over Destruction, Light over Darkness, and above all, in the person of the prince who would become king, of Divinely Ordained Rule over the land of France. And the land of *la France* was to be symbolized in the person of a most radiant and lovely woman, who would join the king-to-be in a brilliant dance at the end of the ballet."

I stare at a thin mist rising off the water and try to imagine what Chrétien is describing.

"When the day came for the ballet to be presented, the nobles believed, as the prince sought they should, that the part of *la France* was undertaken by a boy dressed in woman's clothing, as was considered then most proper. However, the part was danced in truth by Marie-Anne, for the prince declared he would not disgrace *la France* by having the embodiment of the nation poorly danced by anyone else.

"Marie-Anne danced the role to perfection, but when the ballet was concluded at the stroke of midnight, she shed her fine garments and her golden slippers and arrayed herself in the ordinary garments of a member of the servant class so that no one should know the part had been played by a woman and not a boy. For this would have been a revelation both dangerous to herself and compromising to his majesty.

"His majesty the prince was dismayed, however, not to find Marie-Anne following his triumphant ballet, especially when, to a person, the nobles of France asked who had so regally portrayed *la France* in the ballet. But Louis, rather than voicing his dismay at the disappearance of the girl, would not remark upon her at all. Rather, he shook his head and replied, *I am France; is it seemly you should demand any other?"*

I grin. I actually ran across a similar saying of Louis Quatorze: *"L'etat, c'est moi."* Roughly, "I am the nation."

"But in his own heart," continues Chrétien, "the prince was distressed that Marie-Anne had so thoroughly hidden herself from him, both that night and in the days that followed. He advertised throughout the players and singers who had performed with him, declaring he must speak to the *danseur* who portrayed *la France*. Only a few of Marie-Anne's closest associates knew the truth: that 'he' was

145

a girl.

"After several days, seeing that the prince Louis was not to be turned from his search for Marie-Anne, the master of properties of the dance told Marie-Anne to put on her finest gown and her pair of golden dancing slippers and instructed her to go to the prince that evening. This she did, and in the way of a young man whose passion is enflamed, the prince took Marie-Anne is his arms that night and made her all manner of promises, which, in the way of a young man, he kept not.

"But when he learned, months later, that Marie-Anne was no longer well enough to dance, being grown large with his child in her belly, Louis took pity upon the girl and made promises which he was more able to keep. He told her that her child should not lack a father, nor should she lack a husband, if that were acceptable to her.

"And she said a husband possessing a kind heart would be most acceptable, and she agreed to be married to whomever her lord the prince deemed best."

"You," I say softly.

"Yes," says Chrétien. "Myself."

"So, the cinder girl was, uh, *with* the prince," I say. "She just didn't *stay* with the prince."

Chrétien shrugs. "*Monsieur* Perrault, when he wrote down the fairytale, married them in his story. But, in truth, such a marriage would have been the death of the prince's hopes to rule and unite *la France*.

And France was his first and deepest love. He loved Marie-Anne only in passing, as a man loves a beautiful woman for a night of *plaisir*, of pleasure."

"A one-night stand," I murmur. I stare at the shoe in my hand. Cinderella's slipper. "That is *so* the opposite of romantic. I'm glad your friend changed the story when he wrote it down."

Chrétien laughs. "And I am glad my lord the king thought me worthy to be husband to a woman of such extraordinary gifts."

"I guess that was nice of him, considering the times you lived in. I don't remember hearing of any other kings who found husbands for the girls they knocked up."

"It was unusual," agrees Chrétien. "My father tells me Louis Quatorze legitimized as many of his bastard children as he was made aware of and married them to princes and princesses of Europe, to secure lasting alliances."

"Huh," I say. "That's more than my dad ever did. No Christmas presents, no child support, and definitely no arranged marriages to foreign royalty."

Chrétien looks puzzled, uncertain whether to laugh or not.

"Just me trying to turn everything into a joke," I murmur. I grab a pebble off the floor and throw it into the water.

Plink! And then silence.

"Your father, you spoke of him to me one other time," says Chrétien.

"I did?"

"When I told you my father only learned of my existence in my fifteenth year of life, you asked me how that had come to pass."

I very much doubt I said "come to pass," but I let Chrétien continue without me interrupting.

"And then you seemed to recollect yourself and declared my father must have been like your father in that regard."

"It is seriously hilarious to hear you try to repeat what I said."

"But, why?"

"Because I don't speak like a seventeenth century French courtier," I say.

Chrétien looks disappointed. "I have made the endeavor, upon repeated occasions, to render my speech more acceptable to the modern ear. But I seem doomed to failure in this regard."

I try not to laugh at him, which results in this snorting kind of laugh bursting out of me. And then Chrétien is laughing, too, and our laughter is this warm thing that makes the moment stick in my head like it's already past and I'm remembering it far in the future. And I want to so much. Remember today, remember Chrétien, remember our laughter.

"Perhaps we should return," says Chrétien at last. "The moon has traveled already far this night." He points to where the shaft of moonlight spills in silver glory upon a stone in the water which I hadn't noticed before.

"Can we take the shoe back, to show Sam?" I ask.

Chrétien's brows contract briefly, but then he smiles. "But, of course."

I rise, tucking the slipper in a pocket in my sweater. I'm dead-tired, and I know if we ripple, that feeling will disappear along with my flesh and bones. Besides, it's one more chance to hold hands with this remarkable boy. Man. Whatever.

"Chrétien, how old are you? I mean, if you subtract out the years spent invisible."

He smiles. "I believe, *Mademoiselle*, that I exceed your own age by two years."

I whistle, long and slow. "You were a dad at, what, seventeen?"

"Sixteen," he tells me. "Nearly seventeen, though," he adds with a grin.

"That's just way too young," I say.

Chrétien laughs softly, but he doesn't contradict me. And I wonder, as he places his hand in mine and ripples us away, how old my own dad was when he hooked up with my mom. Maybe my dad was young and scared and didn't have a king commanding him by royal decree to stick around.

It doesn't excuse him, but, still, it makes me think.

Chrétien races us back to the cottage. The sky overhead shows no sign of dawn, which is nice because I might actually get a couple hours of sleep this way. Everything's dark and quiet inside the tiny farmhouse. We come solid beside the couch where Will does his noisy sleep-breathing. Sam has curled up beside him sometime in the night. This is saccharinified, but it sort of makes my heart hurt at the same time.

What if having Li genes means I'm not the sort of person who gets to have someone in my life? Someone who sticks with me? None of the aunties are married. One was, but it ended in divorce while they were all still back in Hong Kong. Ma's never seen anyone as far back as I can remember. The Li women are strong and independent, which I admire. But, except for Ma with her cats, they're also alone. And I don't want that for me.

I stumble back past Sam's room. The moon is low in the sky now and it pours through Sam's window onto that cold empty bed. I shiver and tumble into my own bed, next door. I need to think of something nice so I don't have bad dreams. I close my eyes and think about the pool of water underground. About the whisper of moonlight filtering through those holes in the ceiling. About how the crumbling walls made something in me sigh with longing. I pull the shoe out of my pocket and run my thumb along the slippery satin lining.

And just before I fall down into a deep sleep, I remember I've seen that slipper somewhere before.

Chapter Fifteen

THE POISONING PRINCESS

Everyone lets Gwyn sleep in the next morning, for which I can tell you Gwyn is grateful. Very grateful. I am starving when I wake up, though. I'm still dressed from last night, so all I have to do before I devour all the consumables in the farmhouse is slip into some shoes.

My new red shoes.

A smile tugs at my face when I remember Chrétien putting the shoe on my foot back in the village of Vieilles Dames. And no, the parallels between his actions and those of the prince in *Cinderella* are not lost on me.

I shake my head. I have got to get over this boy. I slide my foot into the other shoe, hopping while I get the stubborn back unfolded. And that's when I remember where I saw that golden slipper before.

I stroll out to the kitchen.

"She's awake," says Will.

"Starvation will do that to you," I mumble. "Food. Now."

Chrétien, rising, brings a platter of croissants to me.

I don't bother with butter or jam. I wonder if rippling makes you hungrier than usual. But no, I decide, it's probably just living in the same place as Chrétien that makes me hungrier than usual.

I tear off a fluffy piece of croissant watching his backside as he returns to his seat next to Sir Walter. Unavailability notwithstanding, that boy is a feast for the eyes, especially wearing the jeans Sam and I made him buy yesterday in Carcassonne. The French have definitely improved upon the American art of framing the derrière in denim. Or it could be Chrétien's derrière is simply exceptional all on its own. I shove the remainder of the croissant in my mouth.

"Coffee," I mumble through my mouthful. "Please."

Sam is already on it, passing me a heavenly bowl of half hot milk, half coffee, half sugar. Mathematically impossible, but delicious. I smile and sigh my thanks to Sam.

Then I turn to Will. "Can I borrow your computer?" I ask.

Will slides the computer in front of me, and I attempt to reconstruct a trail I followed earlier. I find the article on "Her Most Christian Majesty, the Dowager Queen of France, Anne of Austria." (And people complain about spelling *my* name!)

There it is: *"Did Louis XIV's Religious Mother Poison Her Son's Lovers?"*

I scan through the article, looking for the link I clicked last time. The first one's a dead end: I don't need to know more about the sexual intrigues of Louis's younger brother, thanks all the same. The second link I try takes me to a page I can't read because it's written in German. I'm pretty sure I didn't have to use Google translate on the article I'm remembering.

I find the right link on my third try: *"The Queen's Trophies: New Evidence Against the Poisoning Princess?"* Well, considering they didn't even bother to get her title right, this may not be the most reliable of articles.

"What's that?" Will asks, leaning into my personal space.

"Stop breathing down my neck," I grumble. "That's what Sam's for." Which earns me a piece of croissant, tossed at me by heretofore-mentioned Sam. Huh. My language is getting Chrétien-ized. That is disturbing. I prefer to be laughed at for my wit, not my word choice.

"This is interesting," says Will, who has ignored my request to breathe elsewhere. "Disturbing if it's true, but interesting, too."

I shoulder him a few inches back. "Dude."

"I take it you're looking at something history-related?" asks Sam, looking over Will's shoulder from his other side.

Will grins. "You *so* get me."

"I don't *get* you," says Sam, "but I know you. Either it's historical or you've developed a crush on Gwyn. Seriously, give her some room, Will."

Will sighs dramatically and nestles his head onto Sam's shoulder instead.

"Please," I mutter. "Order me some chemo, *stat.*"

"Chemo?" asks Sam.

"The saccharine around here is reaching carcinogenic levels."

Sam kisses Will on the mouth.

I roll my eyes to the ceiling. "Are you kidding me?"

"What are you reading about?" Sam asks.

Will's head pops back off her shoulder. "It's a conspiracy theory kind of thing about Anne of Austria, Louis the Fourteenth's mom."

I read the first line out loud. "*A newly-discovered box of treasures with a clear trail back to Queen Anne of France (1601-1666) lends possible support to the rumor the queen may have had a hand in the demise of her son's lovers.*"

Across the table, Chrétien snorts in indignation. "Who dares suggest such a thing?"

"Those who find it too great a trouble to publish their findings in rigorous academic journals," says Sir Walter.

"The article is nothing but 'may haves' and 'possiblies,'" says Will.

"The imaginings of someone in pursuit of what I believe you call a 'quick buck,'" says Sir Walter.

"But look at this," I say. I point to the picture that is the whole reason I wanted to find the article in the first place.

"The shoe?" asks Sam.

I nod. But then it occurs to me I don't have Chrétien's permission to share the story he told me. I mean, for me, it's an interesting story. For him, it's a tragedy. A possibly *fresh* tragedy.

"Chrétien, maybe I should talk to you about this," I say quietly.

"Come on, Will," says Sam. "Let's find out how walking feels on that leg of yours today."

I smile at her, grateful for her kindness *and* her psychic powers.

Chrétien sits down beside me, curious.

"I didn't want to mention the story you told me," I murmur softly. "Not without your permission."

A soft inhale of breath at my side. His hand clenched into a fist. He looks at the picture, considers the article.

"This is preposterous," he says, his contempt clear. "A fantasy spun of deceit."

Sir Walter's head inclines to one side, and his right eyebrow lifts. French for, *"Tell me more,"* if I had to hazard a guess.

Chrétien's mutterings switch to French and I catch a lot of "never" and "good queen" and "horrible journalists."

155

Sir Walter rises and crosses to our side of the table.

"Ah," he says, once he's looking over our shoulders. "Is that not the slipper worn once upon a time by your fair wife?"

The picture on the screen shows "*a single golden shoe, a jeweled comb, a snuff box, and an ivory busk-bone, among other things,*" according to the article. The writer claims the queen, who was very pious, kept these things to remind her to pray for her sins. Which does sound a little bogus, if you ask me. I mean, commit murder, repeatedly, and then keep trophies so you don't forget to ask for forgiveness?

Chrétien looks distressed now. He's got both his hands in tight fists and he's running his thumbs back and forth along his folded knuckles. I feel awful.

"I'm sorry, Chrétien," I whisper.

"Not at all, *Mademoiselle,*" he says. He straightens and seems to collect himself. "I would be a fool to be disturbed by mad imaginings such as these." He turns to me, smiling. "As for the slipper of gold, you were correct. That box, wherever it lies, contains the twin of the shoe you last night held within your own hand."

"Why'd you only keep one of them?" I ask Chrétien.

He smiles sadly. His gaze falls on the table, but it looks to me like his mind is far, far away. "There was *ma mère,* my mother, to be provided for when I chose to no longer remain … in the realm of the visible. I wished to keep something of Marie-Anne's always with me, but I left its mate with my mother. I told her, should she grow desperate, that *la reine*, the dowager queen, would ransom the slipper for the sake of Madeleine."

"For Madeleine's sake?" I ask. "Don't you mean for Marie-Anne's sake?"

Chrétien shakes his head. "The queen loved Madeleine, who was her first ... how do you say, *petite enfante*."

"Her first grandchild," I say, my voice soft.

"Indeed," Chrétien says with a small bow. "And so you see how it is impossible I should believe these slanders against Her Majesty, Queen Anne." He bows and walks away.

I close the window on the computer. My face feels hot and I want to apologize all over again.

Chrétien occupies himself poking at the fire, convincing the half-burned logs to flame a bit brighter. I am trying to figure out how to proceed in the "Cheer Chrétien Up" department when Pfeffer pops into existence out of thin air, along with Mickie.

"Knock much?" I mutter to myself.

"Waldhart," Pfeffer says, addressing Sir Walter by a name none of the rest of us use, "We may have a problem."

"With some of Helmann's 'sleepers,'" says Mickie.

Chapter Sixteen

CIVIL RIGHTS

One of über bad guy's kids is causing problems? There's a big surprise.

"Where's Will?" Mickie demands, looking around the room.

"Out walking with Sam," I say.

Mickie nods and the worry leaves her face.

"I received a call from Martina," says Pfeffer.

I recognize the name. She's one of the first group of five sleeping ripplers woken by Sir Walter with Helmann's secret pass phrase.

"Martina says Georg and Hansel didn't show up at the clinic today," says Mickie.

"Why is that bad?" I whisper to Chrétien.

"*Mademoiselle* Mackenzie and *Monsieur* Pfeffer have made it possible for the 'sleepers' to work as volunteers in Montpellier," he replies. "If they have disappeared ... it doesn't bode well."

Pfeffer continues. "Martina says the two have been making disparaging remarks about the work to which they are relegated, and she is afraid they may have left for good."

"So?" I ask. It doesn't sound that bad to me. "If there's one thing I know about volunteering, it's that you don't want people who don't want to be there in the first place."

"If they go rogue," Mickie says, "who's to say what they might get involved with. They can turn *invisible*."

"No," says Pfeffer. "That is, not at first, at least."

"Oh," says Mick. "That's true."

"Why can't they ripple?" I ask.

"Pfeff's been dosing them with Neuroprine," Mickie explains. "The drug invented to suppress rippling over the long term, as opposed to Neuroplex, the drug which instantly but temporarily stops rippling."

I frown. "Is that legal? Because it sure sounds like a violation of civil rights to me."

Mickie scowls at me. But if there's one thing I've learned about Mickie-scowls, they show up when she knows you have a point.

Sir Walter speaks. "It may be, *Mademoiselle* Gwyn. We are treading upon dangerous ground no matter what we do. If we leave *les anges*, the Angels, to sleep, are we not culpable? If we release them unto the world to choose their own way and they choose to do evil, are we then culpable? With great difficulty, Pfeffer and I have agreed it would be best to learn more of them, as individual souls, before allowing them to exercise their power."

"Well, maybe they didn't like that, and that's why they took off," I mutter, my arms crossed.

"Oh," says Mickie, softly, covering her mouth with one hand.

We all stare at her.

"What if they didn't take off at all?" she whispers.

"*Mademoiselle?*" asks Sir Walter.

"What if Fritz kidnapped them because he wasn't getting anywhere by asking you to swap the journals?"

Sir Walter frowns.

I wrap my arms tightly around my torso.

Chrétien whispers to me, "Are you unwell?"

"Just a little sensitive about anything kidnapping-related," I reply.

"How badly do we think Fritz wants that black book of Helmann's?" asks Mickie. "Bad enough to kidnap someone?"

"If Fritz has, indeed, surmised his father's pass phrase is hidden in one of the journals, he might do worse than kidnapping," says Pfeffer. "He is a coward, but he is as ruthless as any of his siblings."

"So you think he wants to wake up the sleeper agents?" asks Mickie.

Pfeffer shrugs. "I can't be certain. Of all Helmann's children, Fritz was the most secretive. He never opposed his father, but I confess I do not know what his ambitions might be."

"Does he perhaps seek an army?" asks Chrétien. "The sleepers would present a formidable army, could they be persuaded to follow Fritz."

"They were raised to value compassion," says Mickie. "You read the journal. Helmann culled the herd of any who weren't willing to run into burning buildings to rescue kittens, that sort of thing."

"He did, indeed," says Sir Walter, tugging at his goatee.

"But Helmann was able to use those instincts to convince them to do harm," says Pfeffer. "Fritz is adept at spinning the truth—he could do what his father did."

We sit in silence for a minute. The fire pops loudly, sending an ember onto the carpet. Chrétien kicks it swiftly back to the hearth, checking for additional sparks.

Sir Walter paces and speaks again. "I am not, on reflection, inclined to suspect Fritz has stolen them away."

"Why not?" asks Mickie.

"Had he done so, my cousin would be likely to gloat over such an action," replies Sir Walter. "And, of course, to threaten us with their demise. Yet we have not heard from him."

Pfeffer nods. "You're right about the gloating. Fritz can't resist making the most of instances where he holds the upper hand. Such instances came rarely while his siblings lived."

"Maybe Fritz didn't have to kidnap them," I say.

"What is your meaning, *Mademoiselle?*" Chrétien asks.

"If you guys are all busy denying their civil rights, maybe Hansel and Gretel decided to join up with Fritz on their own."

"Georg," murmurs Chrétien.

"Surely not," says Sir Walter.

I shrug. It sounds pretty plausible to me.

Pfeffer frowns, rubbing his hand over his mouth.

"Pfeffer?" asks Sir Walter. "You are concerned?"

Dr. Pfeffer returns his hand to his side and chews his lower lip instead.

"Well," he says after a few seconds, "they knew their 'Uncle Fritz' from his frequent visits to deliver their inoculations." Pfeffer turns to me. "We were not the first to inoculate the sleepers so that they could not disappear. Helmann did so as well, from the time they first demonstrated the ability to ripple until shortly before he placed them in hypnotic sleep. Rippling freely was only allowed a few times a year, and only for training. In addition, had they chosen to run off, they were informed they would perish, as Helmann had made certain they all carried a genetic trait designed to make them ill, should they not return for their 'medicine.'"

"For real?" I ask.

Pfeffer nods. "They will fall ill without receiving an enzyme they are each unable to produce."

"Like the dinosaurs in Jurassic Park," Mickie adds.

I nod. Even though I was too much of a chicken to watch Jurassic Park when I was a kid, I still get the basic idea.

"Well," says Sir Walter, "If I might make a suggestion, I believe we should not let our minds run wild with fears that may never materialize."

"Perhaps," says Pfeffer. "But we must remain vigilant for reports which might indicate the presence of rogue ripplers in ..." Pfeffer consults his watch, which must have a calendar on it. "In eight days time."

"Or less, if they pay a visit to Uncle Fritz," says Mickie. "Didn't you say he cooked up an antidote?"

"Yes," says Sir Walter, frowning. "To counteract Neuroplex."

Sam and Will push through the front door as Sir Walter finishes speaking. The two of them glance around the room, taking in our serious-looking faces.

"What's wrong?" asks Will.

Mickie explains quickly.

"Someone needs to go talk to Martina in person," Will says. "I volunteer."

"You're not going anywhere," snaps Mickie. "Broken leg, much?"

Will shrugs. "Over-protective, much?"

"Someone should go," Sam says. "Don't you think, Sir Walter?"

Sir Walter sighs and gives his goatee one final pull. "I shall accompany Dr. Pfeffer," he says.

163

"*Mademoiselle* Mackenzie, would you be so good as to come along with us?"

Will gives his sister a hug around one shoulder.

"Stay out of trouble," she says to him. "Same goes for the rest of you," she adds, looking at me, Chrétien and Sam.

"You're turning into one big fluffy marshmallow," says Will, hugging her tighter.

"Hmmph," Mickie grunts.

"Might I accompany you as well?" asks Chrétien. "While some of the Angels found my manners strange, I believe Martina trusted me."

Mickie nods. "That's true. She did."

"Chrétien, you should go," says Sam. "If Martina connected better with you, she might be willing to tell you things she wouldn't tell Mick or Pfeff. I mean, she'd be ratting on the siblings she grew up with. That takes some trust, right?"

Sir Walter gives his mini-beard a few mini-tugs while staring at me. He looks worried. Because of me. The Muggle.

"Look," I say. "I don't need a babysitter."

"She'll be fine with me and Will here," says Sam.

"Who would even know where to find us?" I ask. "No one, right?"

Sir Walter nods and the four of them ripple invisible, leaving us alone in the isolated farmhouse.

Chapter Seventeen

ENSORCELLING

Will yawns loudly. "Okay, that walk did me in. Sam, you mind if I crash in your room?"

"Go ahead," she says, giving him a quick kiss on the cheek.

For a moment, I expect her to follow him back, but she doesn't.

"He didn't sleep well," Sam says to me. "He wanted to quit taking pain killers, so he tried it last night, but his leg is still pretty sore."

I nod.

"How are you doing?" she asks me.

"Me? I'm fine."

She tilts her head and pulls her mouth into a line that says *I don't believe you.*

I sink onto the couch beside her, groaning

dramatically. "What do you expect? In the last six days I've been kidnapped, drugged, held as a criminal trying to flee France without proper documentation, and forced into a closer relationship with the hottest guy to walk the face of the Earth in over three centuries."

"You forgot about being held at gunpoint with the safety off," says Sam.

"Right. That, too."

"Well, when you put it that way," Sam says, struggling to keep a straight face.

"I know, right?" I try to keep a straight face, too.

We stare at each other and then start busting up, giggling like middle-schoolers. Sam catches herself first, nodding toward the hall.

"Will's trying to sleep," she says.

We quiet down and I kick my shoes off, drawing my feet up onto the couch so I can hug my knees.

"Oh, Sam," I say in a voice just above a whisper.

"What?"

I shake my head.

"Tell me," she says.

I drop my chin onto my knees and then twist my face around so I can see both Sam and the fire. The fire's not staring me down with puppy eyes, so I fix my gaze on the bright embers.

"I take it this is about Chrétien?" she asks.

I don't bother to nod. She's psychic, after all.

Sam sighs. I sigh.

"You got any more of that color-changing toe polish?" I ask after a few seconds. "The French stuff that predicts your love life depending on color?"

"You want to paint your nails?"

"I want to know if I'm 'lucky in love' or just 'passionate in love,'" I explain.

"Yeah," says Sam. "It sure would be handy if I had that polish so we could check which one it is."

"You mock my pain," I say. "You're the worst best friend ever."

Sam grunts out a small laugh. "Probably, given my track record."

I frown at her. "You're not still blaming yourself for—"

"No, no, no," she says, interrupting me. "For once, I wasn't."

Neither of us mentions the name of her childhood best friend who was killed by Hans.

"I just meant," Sam continues, "that because of me, you've been put through a lot recently."

"I have a long way to go to catch up to you."

"Oh, Gwyn," says Sam. She brushes a stray hair back off my face.

The simple gesture of kindness does me in, and I groan dramatically.

"You've got it bad, girlfriend," says Sam. She puts her arm around me and scoots closer.

"I've just never met anyone like him," I say.

"Who has, right?" asks Sam.

"It's not just his age," I say. "Or maybe it is. I mean, maybe the seventeenth century was when guys peaked, as a gender."

"Will's okay," says Sam.

"Will's taken."

"Oh," says Sam. "Do you …"

"No," I say sharply. "God, no!"

"Right," says Sam. "I knew that."

"No," I say. "It's Chrétien or no one. And someone beat me to him by a long stretch. So I guess that means I'm screwed."

"Give him some time," says Sam.

"He's had three hundred years," I retort.

"That's not fair."

"The whole thing's not fair," I say.

"Oh, Gwynnie," says Sam.

"I … like him … so much." My voice is wispy and broken.

"I know," she says. "I know." She rubs my back.

"And he's in love with someone who died before the Chinese discovered America. How do I compete with that?"

Sam nods. "It does look pretty bad, when you put it that way."

I groan again.

"Although," she says, "we're going to have to break the news to Will."

"We are?"

"About the Chinese discovering America," she says.

"Shut up," I say. "I meant before the Chinese knew America existed. Obviously."

"Obviously," says Sam. "In fairness, Will loves

reminding me Columbus didn't 'discover' America, either."

We lean our heads together.

"What am I going to do, Sam? I've never felt like this about anyone before."

Sam smiles. "Not even one of the guys you ensorcelled?"

"The guys I ... what?"

"It's a new word I got from Chrétien ," says Sam. "But it describes you perfectly. It means you cast a spell and guys are helpless to resist your powers."

I laugh, a tiny snort. "Guys in this century don't stand a chance against my sorcelling."

"I don't think 'sorcelling' is a word, actually."

"Shut up," I say. "Of course it is. To sorcel: *verb*, transitive. To become ensnared by a member of the species *gwynicus minimus*."

Sam laughs.

"But who cares. The only guy I have ever, *ever* felt this way about doesn't know I exist."

"Um ... I'd say he knows you exist," says Sam.

"You know what I mean," I say.

I don't know the last time I felt this depressed.

Sam hugs me. "I'm so sorry, Gwynnie."

On the other hand, I don't know the last time I felt this cared about, either. I hug her back.

"I should go shower," I say. "Or bathe. Whatever you do in this crazy country."

"There's a shower thingy," says Sam. "It's a nozzle on a hose. You have to hold it up."

"Like I said: crazy."

But I trudge back to the bathroom, shower off, put on make up and clean clothes, and start to feel like life might just be survivable with a thoroughly broken heart.

And that's when we hear the sound of someone driving up. Someone *not* driving Sir Walter's car.

Chapter Eighteen

HANSEL AND GRETEL COME TO CALL

"Will!" Sam whispers loudly as she runs down the short hall. "Will, wake up! Intruders!"

Will snaps to and Sam says, "I've got Gwyn. There's no time to hide the fact people are living here. Go!"

Will waits until Sam grabs my hand and ripples us both away to safety. He disappears half a second after us. It occurs to me to wonder if Sam and I will be able to "talk" or not.

A second later, I see something. Something *superimposed* over my regular perception of the world around me. It's a notepad and words are appearing on it. Magic words. Appearing, magically.

Why do I see words on a piece of paper in front of me? I throw the words out there, like I mean for them to be overheard.

A second later, I hear Sam in my head.

You can see that? she asks me.

Yup, I reply.

And you hear me?

No, I answer. *You're totally imagining my voice in your head right now.*

Sam is silent for a second. The note pad continues filling with words.

Say something only Gwyn could say. Something in Chinese.

Sam, I say, *you're being a total dweeb.*

That works, she says. *Will can't hear me, so we write each other. Because we can each see images from one another's heads. I don't know if you're seeing stuff from Will's head or my head.*

A message appears in shouty-caps on the notepad.
HELLO—STRANGER DANGER ALERT!

Sam replies. *Sorry! Gwyn can hear me and see your messages.*

SERIOUSLY?

I guess Will forgot to turn off the shouty-caps.

WE'LL FIGURE THAT OUT LATER, he writes. *FOR NOW, HIDE IN THE WALLS. JUST IN CASE.*

Just in case *what,* I want to ask, but I feel Sam pulling us into a wall. It's tickly, like before, but the tickle sort of dies down to a nice magic-fingers massage after a minute.

The intruders, visitors, whatever, are shuffling

around on the gravel drive. They knock at the door.

Not bad guys, I say. *Just visitors.* I am hoping that if I say this, it will make it true. But a second later, the door swings open. Two men enter and one is holding a firearm. But it's not the carrying of weapons that is the problem. Both the dudes bear an uncanny resemblance to Hans.

COMMUNICATE WITH IMAGES ONLY. JUST IN CASE THESE GUYS CAN "HEAR," Will writes. And then, a moment later, ominously, *IT'S THEM.*

Crap.

Hansel-and-Gretel them? I write.

Yes, Sam replies.

Well, that's just great. At least we know why they didn't show up for volunteer work today. They had something better to do. Like break into Sir Walter's super secret farmhouse carrying a weapon. The two blondies whisper.

"Check down the hall," says the one with the gun.

HANSEL, writes Will.

The other one takes off down the hall, passing us where we hide in the wall.

Gretel? I ask.

Georg, Sam writes.

Heh, I write. *I like Gretel better. Hey, Sam? Question? If we're inside a wall, how come I can see stuff? Do we have x-ray vision to see through walls?*

Our faces aren't in the wall, Sam writes. *It's a trick Sir Walter taught us—leave your face out so you can see. Because,*

173

no, we don't have x-ray vision.

Too bad, I reply. *I wouldn't mind seeing through Chrétien's—*

GROSS! writes Will.

Oh, I write. *Sorry, Will.*

I swear I can feel Sam rolling her eyes at me.

Gretel scurries back to the main room, shaking his head when Hansel raises his eyebrows in a question.

"No one here, either," says Hansel, now speaking at a normal volume. He sees my red shoes, lying where I kicked them off, and nudges one with his foot, making me very indignant. "There's a fire, so they can't be far."

Or we could be, you know, INVISIBLE, I write.

Gretel walks over to the coffee table and picks up my cell phone. *My* cell phone! He wakes up the screen and opens a few things. I'm so putting password protection on that thing the first chance I get.

"This is the girl's phone. The number matches what headquarters traced."

"San Francisco got something right for once," says Hansel. His tone makes it clear this isn't always the case.

Put my phone down! I shout at them with all my mind meld powers.

Gwyn! What if they can hear us? writes Sam.

Hansel looks up, but it could have been because a spark flew from the fireplace. He kicks the ember back, glancing around.

Guess we'll never know, I reply. Gretel is still messing with my phone, having demonstrated no ability to hear me shouting at him.

THEY FOUND US BY TRACING GWYN'S PHONE? writes Will.

Why are they looking for us? I ask.

Sam replies, *Um, it sounds like they came looking for Gwyn, specifically. San Francisco is where Geneses is headquartered. Considering they came inside with a weapon drawn, I'd guess they're here to kidnap Gwyn again.*

That's not very original, I write.

It was effective, Sam replies. Her "notepad" looks like a cell phone screen. I guess she likes to "text" her messages. Figures Will would go for something more … historically dated.

WE NEED TO LEAVE, Will writes, *IN ORDER TO WARN SIR WALTER THE SAFE HOUSE HAS BEEN BLOWN.*

Wait, Sam writes. *Hansel is texting. Let's see if we can find out more.*

A hundred euros says it's Uncle Fritz behind this, I write.

I'LL GO READ IT, writes Will.

I can feel Sam about to protest. I remind her, *You've got me attached to you. Twice the bulk of one rippler. Didn't you say cold air gives you away to fellow ripplers?*

Sam writes, *I just hate when he gets all, "I'll protect you because you're a girl."*

Maybe, I reply, *he gets that way because he's too afraid of what he'd feel like if anything happened to you, Ms. Femtastic.*

Hmmph.

At that moment, Will shoots us an image of the cell phone screen. The number is a San Francisco area code and the person on the other end is named "Fritz."

I guess that settles the question of who sent them, I write.

Hansel finishes texting and puts his phone in his pocket. "Put the girl's cell back," he says to his companion.

Yeah, I write. *Put the girl's cell back.*

"I guess we'd better disappear," says Hansel.

"Right," says Gretel.

I never liked the story of Hansel and Gretel, I write.

Georg, writes Sam.

Whatever, I reply.

A second later, it becomes clear what kind of "disappearing" they were talking about. The air around Hansel shimmers slightly and he's gone. Gretel takes a few seconds longer, but then he's gone, too.

LET'S GO WARN THE OTHERS, writes Will. *NOW.*

I feel an emotional tug as I look at my red shoes. My *shoes*. That I got with *Chrétien*. And then I think of something else. Back in my room, Cinderella's golden slipper is hiding somewhere in the blankets on my bed. I'm the only one here who knows about it. I should probably suggest we come solid and grab it before we go. Who knows when we'll be back again?

Do we have time to grab anything? I ask Sam.

We should probably just go, she writes. *Will's worried.*

Are we coming back later? I ask Sam.

I doubt it, she replies. *Our cover here has been blown.*

LET'S GO! Will writes.

I should say something about the golden slipper. It's the last tie Chrétien has to his dead wife. Or maybe this is fate. A chance for a final clean break. Chrétien said himself the slipper grounds him in his past. I could ask Sam what she thinks. But I hesitate.

Because here's the thing: if I go back for the shoe, he might never let her go.

Is it something important? Sam asks.

It's nothing, I say. *Let's go.*

I ignore the uncomfortable tug in my belly as Sam scoots us down the wall toward the far end of the farmhouse, past the bedrooms. We pass through the outer wall, and when we reach the main road, I think of something that takes my mind off whatever it is I've just done.

How are we supposed to contact Sir Walter? I ask. *If the bad guys have my cell, they have all of your numbers. Including Sir Walter's. If they're smart enough to trace my cell, are they smart enough to hack our calls?*

No idea, writes Sam. *We better not risk using any of our phones. We'll have to go to Montpellier to find them.*

I DON'T KNOW WHERE THIS CLINIC IS, writes Will. *YOU GUYS?*

I frown. This is going to be a problem. How do you find possibly invisible people at an unknown location?

Chapter Nineteen

MURDERER OF KITTENS

The fact that a solution comes to me before it occurs to either of my rippling-experienced friends makes me feel just a bit smug. Of course, I have no guarantee it will work.

Maybe we don't have to find the clinic, I say to Sam. *We could try shouting for Chrétien in our heads. Right?*

Um, yeah, actually, says Sam. *I should have thought of that.*

A second later, I hear her calling out: *Chrétien! Chrétien! It's really important we talk!*

There's no answer.

WE SHOULD GET MOVING, writes Will.

We should connect hands, replies Sam. I'm guessing she means with Will, since she and I are already holding hands.

178

OKAY, replies Will. *LET'S GO AROUND THE NEXT BEND AND OFF TO THE SIDE OF THE ROAD SO NO ONE SEES.*

A minute later, Sam and I solidify between a couple of olive trees and some tall brush. Will is standing behind a different tree about twenty feet away.

"That's why we have to grab hands," Sam says to me as we cross to join Will. "So no one gets lost."

"Sure," I say, like this is the most natural thing in the world.

We grab hands and *presto!*, we are invisible and attached to each other. One problem down. But I'm worried how we're going to find the others, what with Sam's mind powers failing to catch Chrétien's attention.

I'm about to ask if getting closer to Chrétien will help, but on a whim, I decide to call out to Chrétien myself. I think about his face—those angular cheekbones, that sad half smile. I think of the way his hand in mine is like holding sunlight. And I say, half a sigh, *Chrétien.*

And he answers me.

Gwyn?

Um, yeah. I'm tongue-tied for a few seconds, hearing that voice. Echoes of his stories bounce around in my head and I nearly tell Sam and Will we have to turn around *now* and get that slipper.

Are you well, Mademoiselle *Gwyn?* asks Chrétien.

Oh, we're fine, I say.

179

I am relieved to hear it, says Chrétien. *You sound … strained, as one who carries a great burden.*

A twitch of guilt passes through me. *No*, I say. *No burdens. Everyone's fine. If by fine, you mean, no one fired their gun at us because we were smart enough to get invisible before they found us.*

I beg your pardon? Chrétien sounds worried.

Hansel and Gretel—sorry, Hansel and Georg—came to pay a visit. They seem to have been looking for … well, for me. Or maybe the journal.

You must flee at once, says Chrétien. He's definitely using his worried voice.

Already fleeing, I tell him. *We're on our way to find you, except we don't know how to … um, find you. Oh, and we wanted to warn you not to go back to the farmhouse. Hansel and Gretel might still be hanging out there. It looked like they might be staying awhile, and I'd guess they aren't feeling friendly towards us.*

Your supposition strikes me as an accurate one, says Chrétien. *Allow me to consult my father and then we shall consider how and when to join one another.*

I sort of feel the moment he turns his attention away from me.

Sam, I say. *I found Chrétien.*

You did? She sounds surprised. *How on earth did you do that when I couldn't?*

Good question.

It takes us over an hour to reach the clinic. Sam and Will apologize to me that they aren't as fast as Chrétien when it comes to invisible motion.

I'll just say, for the record, that this clinic isn't located in one of the prettier parts of Montpellier. When we arrive there, Sir Walter decides it would be bad for us to materialize in the actual clinic.

My father fears someone may be watching for your appearance, Mademoiselle *Gwyn, or that of* Mademoiselle *Sam or* Monsieur *Will,* Chrétien tells me. *Do you see the building to the south of the clinic?*

The one with boarded up windows? I ask.

Indeed. Materialize within those walls. The building is without occupants.

Yeah, I reply, *the boarded up windows were sort of a clue.*

Will writes that I should pay extra close attention because he's taking us through the windows instead of the door.

THE GLASS WILL BE THE SECOND THING YOU FEEL, AFTER THE WOOD. IT'S REALLY COOL. GLASS, I MEAN. HOPE YOU ENJOY!

I have no clue why he thinks I would enjoy rippling through glass. Solid objects and Gwyn should really not cross paths, in my own humble. But when we go through the window-board combination, I feel something like a sort of warm, viscous hug.

COOL, RIGHT? asks Will.

Sure, I write.

A moment later we come solid. Sir Walter and Chrétien, along with Mickie and Pfeffer, appear seconds later.

"*Mademoiselle* Samantha, *Mademoiselle* Gwyn, my

dear Will," says Sir Walter. "I am so greatly relieved to see you are all well."

"So," Sam says, "I guess this answers the question as to whether or not Hansel and Georg are returning to the clinic anytime soon."

"Hansel and Gretel—sorry, Georg—will both get sick, though, right?" I ask. "Without whatever enzyme thingies they need?"

"Fritz can take care of that," Will says.

"Oh," I say. "Right."

Mickie shakes her head. "They seemed so … dedicated."

"Martina did not believe so," says Chrétien. "She felt they had been keeping secrets for some time. She feared they might strike out alone."

Mickie's eyes narrow. "She really *did* tell you more than she let on to me or Pfeff," she says to Chrétien.

"Martina finds me congenial," says Chrétien in response.

Yeah, I'll bet she does. I shake the thought off. "Do Martina and the others seem like they're going to switch to the dark side, too?"

"Martina is very confused," says Chrétien. "It is troubling to awaken within a world which operates not according to what you have deemed 'normal.'"

He's speaking from experience, obviously. My heart pinches. Is he … into Martina? With her blonde hair and blue eyes and displaced-ness?

"I have spoken to the others candidly about what I believe Fritz might want them for," says Pfeffer. "I do not believe the three who remain will attempt to join him." He looks like he's about to add more, but his cell has been making noise from some notification setting. He frowns and pulls it from his pocket.

"It's Fritz," he says. "Another emailed video."

We don't have Will's computer anymore, so we all huddle around Pfeffer's cell phone and watch the newest from Uncle Fritz.

He's holding a cat. A very affectionate and very fluffy cat. Why would any cat want to be friends with a bad guy? *This* cat clearly has bad taste.

Greetings, friends, says our not-friend. The cat in his arms yowls pitifully, begging for more attention by bumping the hand that stopped petting him a moment ago. That fluff-ball looks just like my cat Rufus Sewell, another total pushover who will rub up against anything with a heartbeat.

I am sorry it has come to this, says Fritz. *It would appear you have determined to reject my proposed trade.*

He takes a moment to look around, surveying his surroundings. *Do you know, this area of California is really quite lovely as we approach the Spring equinox.*

It doesn't look much like San Francisco. Not that you can tell from seeing him seated at a table in front of some old brick building.

Well, I'm sure you will want to know what brings me to this charming foothill town.

The camera pans back a little. Sam gasps half a second before I do. Fritz is sitting across the street from the Las Abuelitas Bakery Café.

"That's my cat!" I shout. "That's my cat!" I say again. My brain can't seem to come up with any other words. I feel like a firework must feel in the presence of a lit match.

I wonder if you remember, brother dear, the year Father brought us that litter of kittens? Yes, I'm sure you must. It was the first time he gave us an assignment to engage in active killing. As opposed to, you know, allowing nature to take its course amongst us. I learned an important lesson that winter. Besides how to kill cats, of course. I learned, my dear Pfeffer, that there are some tasks which are less dangerous than others. Ending the life of a cat is a very low-risk proposition, you see.

I feel sick to my stomach. I want to look away, but I can't.

Fighting Franz, on the other hand, was a very high risk proposition. Nasty temper, he had, that boy. Cross him with a fist and you could be sure to expect repayment in double or triple. Do you remember how I convinced Franz to become a sort of personal bodyguard for me? He did not wish to kill his kitten. So we made a deal. His fists to protect me when I needed it in exchange for my ... disposal of the kitten he was assigned to kill.

It's so simple, ending the life of a kitten.

Fritz places one hand around the neck of my cat.

I wonder if I can remember how to do it after all these years.

I gasp.

He shifts his other hand quickly. But Rufus Sewell is faster. My heroic fluff-ball cat claws and bites Fritz before making an escape.

Ah, there he goes, says Fritz, smiling placidly. *So friendly. Everyone in Las Abuelitas has been remarkably friendly. You could learn a thing or two from the people here, Pfeffer. I wonder at your betrayal, after all we've been through together, brother.*

Fritz shakes his head.

Beside me, Pfeffer makes a noise indicating disgust.

After all those years … Well, it can't be helped, I suppose. We went our separate ways. But I think we both want the same outcome from this little … situation.

Fritz pauses and smiles. The camera pans over to Las ABC.

I should hurry with that journal, if I were you, Pfeffer. My patience begins to wear thin. I don't think you want to know what I have in mind for this sleepy little town. You were always a bit of a softie. Refused to kill your kitten as well, didn't you? Father thought you'd outgrown that softness of late, but I knew better. I never trusted you, Pfeffer. And I never liked you, either. So I'll have no qualms about harming those you care for, will I?

Consider this a warning. You have four hours to respond. Then we can discuss how the exchange will be managed.

Oh, yes, brother … about that exchange? This time I promise I will have something you will want.

The video ends.

I want to scream. I want to kick something down. I don't even know all the things I want right now.

"How fast can you get us to Las Abuelitas?" I ask Chrétien.

Chapter Twenty

DON'T TELL ME EVERYTHING WILL BE FINE

Chrétien has yet to figure out how to move more swiftly than a jet airplane, so we're stuck using that form of transportation to get back home. Fortunately, Sir Walter has the means to hire a private one, which will save us a few hours. Chrétien and I board invisibly, to keep the *gouvernement français* from demanding passports neither of us possess.

For me, the flight is one nauseating hour after another. I can't stay asleep—I have nightmares starring Fritz Gottlieb. I see him setting the cat kennels on fire. I see him shooting Ma and the aunties. I even dreams he has an earthquake machine, like some James Bond evil mastermind, and he uses it to shake California off into the sea.

I give up trying to sleep, but I can't stand my

thoughts while I'm awake, either.

Sam and Will are curled around one another in the seats across from mine. Doesn't look like they're troubled with bad dreams. Sir Walter appears to have fallen asleep too, his head resting against the tiny window beside his seat. Mickie and Pfeffer are arguing about what Fritz is most likely to do next.

"Fritz is a coward," insists Pfeffer. "It's his defining characteristic."

Mickie makes a raspberry noise. She's read the journal chronicling Pfeffer and Fritz's childhood so often that she's probably memorized it.

"What do you take for his defining traits, then?" asks Pfeffer.

"I agree, he's a coward," says Mickie. "But he's a sadist, too."

"Not as bad a one as was Hans," says Pfeffer. He stares out his window as if remembering.

"Don't go there," Mickie says, her voice softer, and so quiet I almost don't hear it.

Pfeffer hears, though. He runs a hand over his face like he can wipe off the memories.

"It doesn't matter, anyway," says Mick. "Which evil trait comes out on top. The thing that's important is that we know he's more likely to rely on coercing others to do anything dangerous, as opposed to standing there himself and holding the gun. Or needle. Or whatever."

Pfeffer grunts in a way that means he agrees.

I wish I could sleep without the bad dreams. I

twist in my seat, trying to find a more comfortable position.

"*Mademoiselle,*" says Chrétien, "I think you do yourself no favor to attend to the conversation between *Mademoiselle* Mackenzie and *Monsieur* Pfeffer."

"Next you'll be telling me there's nothing to worry about," I say, folding my arms.

Chrétien frowns. "But there is a great deal to worry about."

"Thanks for trying to make me feel better," I retort. I feel bad immediately. He *was* trying to be helpful.

"Why an untruth would be employed in such a situation is, I confess, beyond my understanding," says Chrétien, his voice soft.

My cheeks flush. "I'm sorry. You're not the kind of person who would lie to make me feel better."

"I would never."

I know this. It's something I like about Chrétien. "I can't stand it when someone won't give it to me straight. It's as bad as lying, in my opinion."

Chrétien's mouth pulls into half a smile. It is slightly off, this smile.

"What?" I demand. "Telling partials truths is every bit as bad as lying."

He does one of those very French shrugs that can mean a million things.

"Oh," I say, thinking of something. "I suppose you had to lie and flatter at court all the time, huh?"

"Indeed, *Mademoiselle*, upon my honor, I did not."

"Will told me courts were all about the flattery."

"He is correct, speaking in the most general of terms," says Chrétien.

"So, why the strong reaction to what I said?"

Chrétien is quiet for a moment, his eyes fixed on something outside the window. When he speaks again, it doesn't, at first, seem to be in answer to my question. "I am no believer in the encouragement of false hope. Especially in a situation such as our present one. However, I am quite persuaded of the value of distraction. Would *Mademoiselle* care to hear a story?"

"Is that a trick question?"

Chrétien smiles and begins.

Chapter Twenty-One

THE BRAVE LITTLE TAILOR

Once upon a time there was an enchanter of men who was very beautiful but also very selfish. And when one day she learned she would give birth to a child, she swore an oath never to reveal to the child that it had a father at all. A father, she knew, might in time take the child from her. Whereas if the child remained and was a girl, the enchantress might train the girl in her own arts and could perhaps leave off from her life of weaving spells over the hearts of men.

As it happened, the child was a boy. "Ah, well," she said to herself, "a boy-child has no magic that I might train him in my own arts, but he can be taught to draw water and tend fires and mend things."

So she raised the boy until he was seven years of age, at which point she apprenticed him to a tailor who made garments which could transform a beggar into a courtier. The boy worked long hours, plying his needle, and at times he fell asleep cross-legged, for you know tailors sit always thus upon their benches.

The boy grew at this time into something of a braggart, for he felt keenly the lack of a father in his life, for other children had both fathers and mothers, but the little apprentice had only the enchantress for a parent. And so, upon any occasion where the apprentice knew himself to have done well, he broadcast his deed far and wide, often embellishing the tale even as he might embroider milord's cloak or milady's overskirt.

One day, he struck two rats which were in the habit of passing through the sewing room and thence through a hole in the wall and into the house of the baker, who dwelt next door. Two vermin in a single blow! Why, that was more than he had heard tell before of anyone doing. And besides, were he to tell the baker, perhaps the baker might make a present of a loaf or pastry or even a cake.

Just to make sure of the present, the apprentice thought he would add unto the tale of his deed another rat to the number of those he killed.

"Three did I strike down with one blow!" he cried as he told his tale to the baker.

"Three of the nasty little vermin? At once?" asked the baker, in some wonder.

The boy, upon beholding all the mouthwatering cakes, thought to make himself more certain of his reward. "Three, sir, or perhaps it was indeed four. The light was not good and my eyes are at all times strained from sewing all the long day."

"Three or four, say you?" The baker nodded. "Well, you shall have both thanks and a reward from me, lad. Only eight years of age, and to strike down four enemies in one blow!"

191

The boy smiled, licking his chops and imagining which of the cakes he would accept when he was given the chance.

"But let us see these foul vermin, that we make be certain they are killed indeed," said the baker.

Now, the boy paled, for he had not considered how, perhaps, there might be occasion for the proof of the three or four dead bodies. Nevertheless, he bade the baker come and see for himself.

And when the baker had stepped into the tailor's shop, he saw for himself two dead vermin. The boy now prepared to swallow his pride and declare that in truth, he had only struck down two rats.

But the baker, upon seeing the two, sighed and said, "Ah, it would seem Mistress Cat has claimed two for herself already."

The apprentice, hungering still for the cakes, decided that allowing someone else to invent a lie was not so damning a sin as inventing the lie oneself, so he shrugged and, when it was offered, accepted his cake.

But, being accustomed to plain food, the cake only made the boy ill, which ought to have perhaps stirred him into a full confession of the truth, but it did not.

The baker, meanwhile, boasted of the boy's prowess to the tailor, who boasted of it to the cobbler, who boasted of it to the tapster, and with each telling, the tale grew a bit grander. One day, as the apprentice sewed upon his bench, he heard the tapster telling milord the baron that the tailor's apprentice struck one day seven vile creatures dead with one blow.

Now, milord the baron smiled at the lad, patted the boy's head, and said such a strong lad should have lessons in the art of war as well as that of the needle. The tailor demanded who *should then do the boy's work, and there seemed to be an end of it.*

But the next week, the tailor told the little apprentice that a sum of gold had been paid so that the apprentice might spend a small portion of every day learning the arts of war for a year and a day. And all this came to pass because of two dead rats and a few lies.

But the tailor warned the boy that milord the baron would expect to see results as surely as he, the tailor, expected to see them when once an investment had been made in a boy's training. At this, the boy grew fearful, but the tailor explained milord would come back in a year, or perhaps two, so that there would be time for the boy to prove he had studied with care.

At the end of the first year, milord returned and demanded to examine the boy's progress in dancing and fencing and riding. Milord was pleased and praised the boy.

"I see I was right to pay for your training. Some day, the boy who struck seven vermin with one blow may do more in service of his village, should enemies attack."

The boy, meanwhile, had suffered greatly in his heart from the lie, and determined to tell milord the truth. And when he had done so, milord the baron stroked his beard thoughtfully.

"I see you have learned more than the arts of needle and sword," said milord. "You have learned also the cost to the soul of telling an untruth. For allowing an untruth to be told and making no effort to correct it is as grave a sin as to tell it oneself."

"Is it?" asked the boy. "Then I am a very great sinner." And he hung his head. For now milord would not wish to have anything further to do with the boy.

But milord the baron stroked his beard once more and replied, "We are all of us great sinners, but we may try to rise above our own propensities to evil. What say you to a bargain between us two: let us keep careful watch upon our tongues this twelve-month and a day. In a year, when I return for the hunt, we shall both make account to one another of any untruths we utter. In addition, because you have valued the truth, I shall pay for another year's lessons in the arts of war."

The apprentice, for all that his mother was a honey-tongued enchanter of men, could only nod, dumbstruck that milord had offered kindness instead of contempt. And the boy made a vow to speak only the truth, neither more nor less, for the twelve-month and a day until milord returned.

He kept his word, both that year, and the year following, and the year following, until he had completed his fourteenth year. Milord the baron returned every year, smiling when the boy passed him in stature, and striking with the boy every year the same bargain: tell no lies, and I shall pay for your training in the deadly arts for another year.

Now, it was not easy for the boy, for many times a lie rises more easily to the tongue than the truth, but he guarded his tongue carefully, and came to be known as a plainspoken young man who could be trusted. And this was, to him, more precious than all the baker's cakes.

As he approached manhood, the apprentice thought and thought, wondering how he might show his gratitude to milord the baron for the valuable gifts he had been given.

And one day, when milord was making his yearly visit, the opportunity presented itself. The baron had asked for a demonstration of the boy's skills, such as they were, and so the two had struck out from the village where the boy could more readily demonstrate what he had learned of dancing, sword-play, and riding.

Milord praised the boy when the demonstrations had been concluded, but he was honest as well. "You are not as skilled as one who has devoted his whole days to the pursuit of these arts, but you have a good eye and carry yourself well on foot and on horse."

The boy laughed, for he knew his horsemanship to be most appalling, having only an old nag to train upon. The two sat down to eat bread and cheese together with the great forest at their backs and the sun upon their faces. And after a time, milord, who had been drinking sweet wine as well, grew drowsy in the sun and slept. The boy sat idly for awhile and grew drowsy himself, and was just upon the point of falling asleep when he heard the thunderous approach of a wild boar.

"Wake, sir, awake!" he cried to milord.

The baron, however, would not rouse.

The boy looked up and counted not one, but three of the great tusked beasts bearing down upon himself and the baron. In great distress, the boy threw his arms about milord and carried them both from the world of substance to the world without substance, which was a gift the boy had, as he believed, from being offspring to an enchantress.

Milord woke, then, and finding himself without substance, cried out with an oath.

The danger having passed, the boy brought himself and the baron back to the world of substance. And milord stared in wonder at his limbs as though to make certain they were all returned.

"What is this you have done?" demanded milord.

Now, the boy was sorely tempted upon this occasion to lie. For his mother the enchantress had warned him he must never speak of his ability to vanish, *"lest they burn you at the stake for accepting gifts from demons."*

But the boy reasoned that if the gift was indeed from a demon, it were better he should risk burning for a short time at the fiery stake than risk burning for eternity in hell, and besides, he had no wish to lie to milord, of whom he had grown very fond.

So, he told the truth to milord, saying he had contracted the ability to vanish shortly after his fifth birthday, and that he did not know from whence the ability came, for his mother disavowed all knowledge of the uncanny gift.

Milord nodded and stroked his beard and said at last that they two must pay a visit to the boy's mother. Now the lad was in great distress, for his mother's trade was a rude on—the enchanting of men's ... hearts—and he was not certain it was right to introduce so great a lord to so mean a dwelling. He spoke his fear, but the baron only nodded and said he would speak with the boy's mother.

When the baron and the enchantress met, they bowed, one to the other, as acquaintances might, and the baron told the boy to depart for an hour. And when the hour had passed, the boy returned to discover the baron in a great rage. But the boy's mother bid him pack his few belongings, for he was to depart and live now with milord.

Now, the boy had no great affection for his mother, with whom he had not lived since before his apprenticeship, but he was distressed to see her in an anger matching milord's own anger.

"Have I done aught to offend, mother, in bringing the baron here?"

"Ask him yourself," said she, "now you are to dwell always with him. But see you forget not your mother in her old age, when one day she loses the art of enchanting men's hearts."

The boy made a vow to remember her and care for her, and departed her house, heavy of heart.

He was, therefore, in a great shock to find himself embraced and kissed many times by milord.

At last, when the baron left off embracing the boy, the boy found the courage to ask wherefore he was to leave his apprenticeship and his mother and his village.

And the baron smiled and said unto him, "Once there was a lord who coupled with a beautiful enchantress, producing, unknown to himself, an heir."

And so the tailor's apprentice became milord's heir, all in consequence of a truth told after the invention of a lie, and they lived happily, father and son, for many years.

Chapter Twenty-Two

THE WORLD IS SO LOVELY A PLACE

Neither of us says anything for several minutes after Chrétien's tale is finished. At last I break the silence.

"It was you, this time, right? The boy in the story?" I ask.

"It was I."

I nod. Of course, a story like that, on top of the million little things I already knew about him, pretty much ruins me for falling in love with anyone else. The bar has been raised, let me tell you.

I speak again. "But that one's a fairytale, too," I say. "*The Brave Little Tailor*, isn't it?"

Chrétien smiles. "Fairytales have all, I believe, their origins in one truth or another."

We're quiet again for awhile, until the silence

starts bugging me.

"Are we there yet?" I ask Chrétien. He pulls his eyes away from the window.

"I beg your pardon?"

"You know, like what little kids say in the car: *Are we there yet?*"

Chrétien looks at me, amused.

"Never mind," I say. I twist again, trying to find a better position. These seats may look comfortable, all leather and pillows, but they're not. Not after six hours, anyway.

"It is incomprehensible to me," says Chrétien, gazing out the window again. "This passage we make through the heavens."

I lean past him and look down. We're not over the ocean anymore, at least. All I see is snowy fields and clouds.

"I never thought to be more than a tailor, when I was a boy," says Chrétien.

The thought of Chrétien sewing clothes all day makes me smile.

"One of my aunties sewed for a living," I say. "Well, they all did, for awhile. Until the bakery business took off."

"Ah," says Chrétien, "to be a baker must be a wonderful thing. To have always at one's fingers items of such delectation."

I laugh.

"What amuses you?"

"You," I say. "I don't even know what you're

saying half the time, I swear."

Chrétien frowns. "My command of your language is pitiable, indeed."

"How do you even know English in the first place? Did Sir Walter teach you once he ... took you in?"

"Indeed, he did not," says Chrétien. "My mother was Anglo-Norman."

He sees the look of confusion on my face.

"English," he adds.

"Oh," I say. "That explains a lot."

"Before I was apprenticed unto the tailor, she taught me both writing and reading, thinking to hire me out as an amanuensis. We had several pages from an English translation of the Bible as well as a bound copy of a play by the English poet, Shakespeare."

"That explains even more."

He looks at me, tilting his head, puzzled.

"I just mean, you sound like some dude out of Shakespeare when you talk."

"Ah," he says.

"You know, old words, funny word order, that kind of thing."

Chrétien smiles. "In my time, the words were new. My lord the king bid me often amuse him with a new word of English."

"Did you have to hide it from the king, how you were a tailor one day and a rich man's son the next?"

Chrétien looks insulted. "But of course I did not attempt to conceal the truth."

"I just thought you might get in trouble. You know, for pretending to be something you weren't."

"I pretended not." He draws his brows together. "From that day in the tale until this day, I have uttered no untruths nor taken any vows I did not also fulfill." Then he smiles. "But indeed, I had no need of concealment at court. My lord the king promoted in my generation many whose origins were humble."

"Really?"

"I hid neither my origins nor my illegitimacy, and the king held neither against me. In fact, he admired my father for acknowledging me."

"I guess he must have," I say. "Seeing as how he acknowledged all his own, um, bastards." I look over to Chrétien. "Is that word offensive?"

"Words are either offensive or not offensive depending on the intent of the one who utters them," says Chrétien.

"Huh," I say. "You may have a point. I don't mind that my eyes are slanted, but I remember crying when kids in Las Abs called me 'slanty-eyes.'"

"But your eyes are wondrous," says Chrétien.

Wondrous?

He catches my gaze and I can't look away. His eyes are full of passion. For a moment I think he's maybe feeling something for me, but then I realize he's probably just angry on my behalf.

I look down and the moment passes. When I glance back at Chrétien, his look is far away.

"I sometimes wonder," he says, "what would

have become of my Madeleine had she lived. She might have been a great princess. Of Spain, perhaps, or of Holland."

"You can't do that," I say.

"What is it I must not attempt?"

"You can't ask 'what if.' It's like Aslan says: *No one is ever told what would have happened.*"

"Aslan?"

"Oh, you never had anyone read you the Narnia books, did you?"

Chrétien shakes his head. "I shall remedy the error at the first possible moment."

I smile. "Good plan."

"Do you believe what you uttered—that there is futility in imagining what might have been?" asks Chrétien.

I shrug. "I believe in what is. Not what might have been. I mean, I like alternate reality timeline stuff as much as the next person, but it doesn't really matter in real life. In real life, you have the hand you were dealt and you have to play it the best you can. 'What if?' is just a colossal time waster."

"You are a most wise female," says Chrétien.

"Girl," I say. "People don't say 'female' nowadays."

"Ah," says Chrétien. "I shall endeavor to remember. My list of to-be-done grows long."

I laugh, but this time I don't correct his usage of modern English. It must be hard to always feel like you don't understand the world you're living in. And our worlds are so different. A nicer Gwyn, a *Gwyn 2.0*, would try to make Chrétien feel more at home, to point out the ways things are the same.

And then I think of one.

"Hey," I say. "Remember when you were telling me King Louis wanted to inspire his people with ballet? To make them feel a part of something larger and more important than their own individual interests?"

"Indeed, *Mademoiselle*."

"Well, I was thinking you should see how people do that in the modern world. I mean, one of the ways. Remember how I told you about flash mobs?"

"The flashing mobs," he says, nodding.

Oh dear. "Um, not *flashing* mobs, just *flash* mobs. Flashing means something else."

Chrétien nods like he's filing this away with "don't call girls *female*."

Sir Walter's jet has wifi, so I show Chrétien some of my favorite flash mob videos. The US Air Force at the Smithsonian, a wedding proposal in Moscow, and, of course, Beethoven in the mall where I used to live.

Chrétien's eyes are streaming tears by the time I've run out of favorites, an hour or so later.

"The world is so lovely a place," he says softly.

Lovely and … other things. I don't say that out loud, though. Some moments are better not spoiled, and every now and again, I have the sense to see it.

Sir Walter's eyes open, and he yawns noisily.

"We land shortly," he says. "It is time to face our

Visible

enemy."

Chapter Twenty-Three

NOTHING SAYS BAKED GOODS LIKE A

SHARP POKE IN THE ARM

There are no air strips in Las Abuelitas, so we deplane just outside Clovis and travel invisibly from there for speed. The road to Las Abs has never felt longer. I'm terrified by thoughts of what we might find when we get there. Sir Walter asks those of us who still have phones to please not use them. Will suggested we could stop in Fresno to hunt down a burner phone so we could call the bakery, but everyone decided the delay in time wasn't worth it.

Which means we're heading to Las Abs blind. And by "heading" I mean speeding along invisibly with me and Sam and Will providing directions to Chrétien, who is at the front of the conga line. We decided to keep everyone connected to everyone else because Chrétien is so much faster moving through the space-time continuum or whatever this is.

We get to the outskirts of town just as the sun is setting, all red and bloated, and quite honestly a bit eerie looking. The inside of Will and Mick's old cabin gives us the cover we need to appear solid without terrifying the good people of Las Abs. I look around the cabin, noticing Ma must have sent the cleaning people over. It's one of her rentals.

"Come on," I say, when Will and Mick start nosing around their former home. "Lives to save here. Let's go!" I'm sick to my stomach with worry, now that we are solid again. I didn't experience the nausea while we were invisible, which makes it seems much worse, now.

"I will report back as soon as I can," says Chrétien.

We picked him to go have an invisible look around, along with Will, before we decide what our next move will be. But I can't stand staying behind.

"Take me along," I say. "Please."

Sir Walter frowns. It's not what we agreed on. He felt it would be safer for Chrétien and Will if I wasn't there having a melt down inside Chrétien's head if, you know, anything bad has happened to my family. Sam's parents aren't in Las Abs at the moment, so there's really only one family Fritz could be targeting.

"I have the right to know," I say quietly.

"Very well," says Sir Walter.

Of course, if he'd said no, I would have grabbed onto Chrétien and Will and refused to let go.

We careen along the highway, past the burnt remains of Sam's old house. Someone's torn everything down to the foundation. I wait to see if Will is going to write something about this, but he doesn't. I guess we're all pretty focused on what we're going to find when we get to Las ABC.

But what we find is ... a normal early evening at the bakery.

It makes no sense, but there's Ma, smiling at customers and handing them bags of goodies, laughing and putting their tips into the Cat Fund jar. I don't see the aunties, but it is pretty obvious to me they must be fine or Ma would not be running the till. At least, I don't think she would. My mom may be a hard-nosed business woman, but even she knows that some things come before business.

We have to pass through the front door, oak on bottom, glass on top, in order to hear what Ma's saying. As Chrétien aims us for an object I know from repeated daily use to be solid, I cringe a little. This time I really notice the glass as it passes over us. It feels like when you pull your hands out of the tub of warm paraffin at the nail salon. Too bad I'm not in a mood where I can enjoy it.

But as I watch Ma from inside, it is clearer than ever that she is fine. Totally fine. I drift through the café in unspeakable relief. Of course, if the aunties are being harmed or threatened in the kitchen at this exact moment, Ma wouldn't know.

Through to the kitchen, I say to Chrétien.

I feel two things when we get into the kitchen, one pleasant and one … not so much. They hit me together, like two people trying to have totally separate conversations with you at a noisy party. The unpleasant thing is the memory of the last time I stood in this kitchen, looking for ways to make Hans back off, and how it didn't work out for me. The pleasant thing is that my aunties are back here, gossiping away in Canton dialect, scooping cookies and torching *crème brulées* for the end-of-day rush about to hit.

They're fine, I say to Chrétien. *Totally fine.*

Chrétien replies. *Perhaps Fritz harmed …* les chats?

The cats! *We better check.*

In my mind's eye, I imagine Fritz standing out back snapping the neck of the last of our fourteen rescue cats. But when we get outside, all I see are fat, happy, snoozing cats everywhere I look.

They're all right, I say to Chrétien. A few of them perk up as we pass by. It's almost like they see us. Rufus, the escape artist who nearly succumbed to Fritz's villainy, starts meowing for attention.

That is so wrong, I say.

To what do you refer? asks Chrétien.

ANIMALS SENSE RIPPLERS, Will writes.

Rufus squeezes out of the kennel and starts flopping around at my invisible feet.

WHAT IS HE DOING? Will asks.

I think he's confused, I reply, writing my answer so

Will can see it. Rufus looks ridiculous, and Woody Allen eyes him with utter feline contempt. *Rufus is trying to find me, only there's no me to find.*

My cat finally gives up in disgust and wanders toward the alley, in search of someone with an actual pulse, I presume.

WE NEED TO CHECK UPSTAIRS, writes Will. *IN CASE FRITZ IS IN HIDING.*

Yeah, 'cause right now what I want more than anything is to find a bad guy hanging in my bedroom.

Will takes the lead, and since I'm attached to Chrétien who is attached to Will, we all proceed *straight up the wall.* No, I didn't make that up. Will takes us up in the air and then through the window-slash-paraffin dip.

Will! We have stairs, you know.

MY WAY IS MORE FUN, he responds.

Chrétien insists we perform a very, very thorough search of the upstairs apartment. I learn that Auntie Sally has taken over my bedroom. (Figures.) Auntie Carrie has spread out in our family room. She probably had Ma's room before Ma came home. But the one thing we can't find any sign of, at all, is Fritz.

Chrétien makes us stand super still and be quiet for three minutes solid to check for "thought signatures" in the area.

I understand not, says Chrétien.

Maybe he changed his mind, I offer.

WE SHOULD GET SOLID AND TALK TO YOUR MOM, writes Will.

Chrétien does his little check that I don't have a foot stuck through the floor, and we come solid, us just after Will.

Will heads for the stairs. "See? I know what stairs are for," he says as he thumps down in his walking cast. "Get your mom to come out back to the kitchen," he says to me. "You can run the till while we ask her a few questions."

"No way," I say, behind him. "I'm not waiting to hear what she says. Auntie Sally can run the till."

After hugs from my startled aunties, Auntie Sally runs out front to get Ma.

"Gwyn!" cries my mom, as soon as the kitchen door is closed behind her. "You're back so soon! Why didn't you call?" Ma asks me about three more questions without waiting for answers. Finally, she shakes her head at me. "If I'd known the French government was going to hurry things up, I could have stayed behind with you."

I don't even mind her going on and on. I am so happy to hear her voice—her actual, annoying, berating voice—that I can only stand there grinning.

"I know, Ma," I say when she is quiet for two seconds straight. "We came without the French government's permission. There's another one of those bad guy brothers still alive and kicking, and he's been making threats, and he was here in Las Abs, and I was so worried I'd never see you again, and—"

Ma interrupts me with the tightest, warmest hug I have ever felt in my life. And I'm wiping a couple of tears off my face and hugging her back. I'm just so relieved everything's going to be okay.

"Can you close early?" I ask. "Sam and Sir Walter and Mickie and Dr. Pfeffer are all waiting for us to report back. They'll want to ask you questions."

"I'm not closing early," says my mom. "Are you kidding? You should see the daily receipts from the last six days." She shakes her head and mumbles a few things in Chinese that aren't exactly complimentary to her big sisters. "You can bring your friends over if you want, but I'm staying open until 6:00 tonight. I should probably get back out there." She casts a glance over her shoulder like Auntie Sally might be doing something very hazardous to the future of Las ABC.

"Ma," I say, "your sister will do fine. She taught you everything you know."

Auntie Carrie clucks in the background, agreeing in Chinese.

Ma rolls her eyes at me and lowers her voice. "We came that close to losing every customer this past week. If it hadn't been for the flu shot sale, I think that new Starbuck's in Oakhurst would have taken all our business."

I don't even want to know what a "flu shot sale" is.

"Okay, so who's going back to get everyone else?" I ask Will and Chrétien.

"Allow me, *Mademoiselle*," says Chrétien.

"What's a 'flu shot sale'?" Will asks after Chrétien disappears.

"I'm sure we don't want to know," I mutter.

"Oh," says Ma, ignoring my mumblings, "it's this great idea a visiting physician had for preventing the spread of influenza this winter."

"Winter's almost over," I say.

Ma shoots me a lids-half-lowered glare. It is so familiar, so *normal,* I could hug her again.

"Anyway," she says, "there was that shortage of flu vaccine between Thanksgiving and New Year's, which is when most people are thinking about flu shots, so by the time the pharmaceutical companies got new batches out to the clinics, most people weren't coming in to get vaccinated."

I yawn. My mom thinks the most boring things are worth explaining in mind-numbing detail. Will, however, is managing to look very engaged in Ma's monologue.

"So this doctor came in for coffee and was explaining the problem, and he took one look at the bakery and said, 'This is the kind of place we need to do flu clinics—where people are already going on their busy days.' So I said, why didn't we do a little vaccination clinic here, where you get your flu shot and then get a free cookie. You know, like they do cookies and juice when you donate blood."

"You gave away juice?" I am shocked because although cookies aren't cheap, juice is *expensive.*

"Are you joking?" asks Ma. "The profit margin on juice is already terrible without me giving it away. We gave away *cookies.* Anyway, it got people coming back in the bakery." Ma leans in close. "Between you and me, my sisters don't get that customer service still means *everything* in a small town. I had to do *something* to get people coming back."

"Yeah, Ma, nothing says warm baked goods like a sharp poke in the arm." My tone is sarcastic, which is something I vowed to cut back on during the flight from France. I flush and then I give Ma a little apology hug.

"Ouch!" she says. "That's the side I got my shot."

"What was the name of the doctor administering the shots?" asks Will.

"I'd have to look. I wrote it down somewhere. Such a nice man. A real humanitarian."

The rest of our group appears, literally. Auntie Carrie waves the *crème brulée* torch at them threateningly, sees they are friendly, and switches to muttering curses in Mandarin. Or maybe she's warding off curses. Hard to tell.

"So nice to see all of you again so soon," says my mom, beaming. She really does like my little group of friends. Of course, they saved my life, so there's that.

"Bridget," says Will, "can I get you to run down the name of that doctor?"

"Sure," she says, frowning slightly. "It was something German. Or Dutch. Danish, maybe."

Will says something I don't catch to Pfeffer, who hands Will his phone. Will pops up one of the Fritz videos.

"Was it this man?"

Ma smiles. "That was him. How are you two acquainted?"

Chapter Twenty-Four

INFECTED

At my mom's confirmation of the worst news ever, Sam covers her mouth and gasps. Will closes his eyes. Mickie swears.

The air in the room seems to whoosh out and my chest feels like a house just landed on it. I cannot take in a breath.

"Someone catch Gwyn," shouts Will.

Four pairs of arms reach out to support me. I didn't even realize my legs had stopped holding me up.

Mickie hands me a paper bag. "Just breathe in and out. I promise it helps."

I bat the bag away. "Ma!" The word comes out in a child's howl of pain.

"It'll be okay," says Sam. "It'll be okay." She turns to Sir Walter, her eyes pleading.

Fritz. I knew it. I knew we wouldn't get off this easy. I try to suck in a breath, but my lungs refuse to cooperate.

"What is the problem with everyone here?" demands my mom. "You're scaring my daughter half to death. Hasn't she been through enough lately?"

"*Madame* Li," says Chrétien, "none of us wishes to increase the discomfort of your beloved daughter. But it is possible something of great danger has occurred."

"Fritz Gottlieb is Helmann's son," says Will. "And he invented the vaccines that killed off entire villages a week ago."

My mother's mouth forms a tiny "o" of shock. "*Wo De Tian A!*" she murmurs.

Auntie Carrie looks over.

"Close the bakery," Ma says to my auntie. "Right now. Tell everyone we're very sorry, but we're closing."

My ancient auntie shuffles through the door from the kitchen to the bakery.

"Tell me what you know," says my mother, looking strong like I have never seen her before. "I need to hear everything."

By the time Sir Walter explains things to my mom, my lungs are working again, and I've shoved the panic away, imagining it as a cold hard knot I can keep in my belly. I swear to myself I will not let my mom and aunties die like this. No one's fallen sick, yet, and that is a lot more promising than what happened in central Africa.

216

Maybe Ma's already had whatever virus was in those inoculations. Maybe Asians are naturally immune. But what about the rest of the people in Las Abs? No one in the café looked ill.

Something's not right here.

"How long did it take for the virus used by the Angel Corps to take effect?" I ask.

Dr. Pfeffer answers. "Between six and ten hours after injection, the victims were dead."

"But Ma's flu clinic was yesterday. Right Ma?"

She nods. "Yesterday 9:00 to noon."

"So," I say, "whatever was in the vaccines, it wasn't the same virus. Or am I missing something?"

"No, *Mademoiselle* Gwyn," says Sir Walter. His eyes widen. "It would appear you have caught something important."

Dr. Pfeffer nods slowly. "It cannot be the same vaccine." His cell phone buzzes and he checks it.

"Another email?" asks Will.

"Yes," replies Pfeffer, terse.

This time, there's no video. Just a written message.

You will respond to me or someone will become very ill. I have randomly injected a toxin into one of the charming Li sisters residing in Las Abuelitas. An antidote exists, but I will only make it available if you deliver my father's journal to me in the next twelve hours. I hope I have made myself clear. If not, someone will die. And that someone will not be the last to die, I can assure you.

Yours,

217

Fritz Gottlieb von Helmann

"We have no choice," says Sir Walter, his voice soft, his gaze unfocused. "He has beaten us."

Ma, who's been quiet up until now, speaks. "One of us is … infected. Or poisoned. Or whatever it is." She speaks in rapid Canton dialect to her sisters. Something about tea. Herbs. Medicine. The aunties nod and the three of them head for the stairs.

Pfeffer, who must know Chinese, calls after Ma. "Until we know what sort of toxin Fritz has used, it would be unwise to complicate things with supplements."

"You handle things your way," I say to Pfeffer, my hands on my hips. "My family will handle things their way."

Pfeffer's mouth shrinks. Then he nods.

"That's my daughter," says Ma, softly.

"Such spirit," murmurs Chrétien.

Ma returns to place a hand on my shoulder. She squeezes tight, and then follows her sisters upstairs.

"What about Fritz?" I ask. "Shouldn't we acknowledge his message?"

Sir Walter nods. "I have been considering our response. I believe we must reply as if we intend to acquiesce."

"It could buy us something valuable," agrees Will. "Time, or information, or cooperation."

"But you can't seriously intend to hand over Helmann's journal, can you?" asks Mickie.

I snap at her. "We will do whatever we have to do

to save a life."

"*Mademoiselle* Mackenzie did not intend to communicate we would do anything less," Sir Walter says, placing a hand upon my arm. "Truly, we will do whatever is needful to save the life that is endangered."

"Fritz believes we have but one journal," says Pfeffer. "And he is uncertain as to whether it contains what he wants."

"It does," says Mickie. "We *know* it does."

"But *he* does not," replies Sir Walter. "What if we were to give him the journal which records the experiments upon his original children?"

"We need that to show the former Angel Corps members," says Mickie. "It's the only proof we have that what we say about Helmann is true."

"Why not give Fritz a fake journal?" I ask. "My auntie Sally can forge anyone's handwriting."

Sam raises an eyebrow.

"She can," I say. "She totally forged the documents that got her and her sisters into Hong Kong following the Cultural Revolution."

"Forgery is out of the question," says Mickie, shaking her head sadly. "Fritz has a lab full of devices which can authenticate the age of the journal, the age of the ink, the presence or lack of presence of Helmann's DNA in sloughed off skin cells, dandruff, that sort of thing. We can't fake all of that."

"In any case," says Sir Walter, "we must not endanger the lives of the Li women by giving Fritz a reason not to trust us."

Mickie sighs heavily. "We have to give up the journal with the experiments. We can't risk him finding the pass phrase in the other one. We'll just have to trust Martina, Günter, and Friedrich will be able to persuade others with the information we gave them."

Pfeffer and Sir Walter exchange glances, both nodding curtly.

"Let us send a conciliatory message to my cousin Fritz," says Sir Walter.

Pfeffer does this, and we wait for what seems like an hour. Although, according to the clock in the kitchen, only ten minutes pass before Pfeffer's cell vibrates with another message.

He holds it up for us to see.

I am so happy you have seen reason, my brother. I will prepare the antidote at once. The exchange will take place in Las Abuelitas. Await my further instructions at the bakery. Don't try anything. I will prepare only enough antidote for one. Once I am completely satisfied as to the genuineness of the item I seek, I will tell you who harbors the toxin. I regret I will not be able to personally attend the exchange. Unfortunately, I don't trust you.

Yours,

Fritz Gottlieb von Helmann

A new fear seizes me. We abandoned everything at the farmhouse when we fled. Did that include the journals? I can't remember if Sam said the journals were safe or not. Weight pushes on my lungs, heavy like the sacks of flour lining one wall of the kitchen. But this time, I push right back.

"Do you have ... the right journal?" I ask Sir Walter.

"Yes," he replies. "I brought the pair of them. I thought it wise."

"It's going to be okay," says Sam, an arm around my shoulder.

I nod. And then the day's events hit me like a hammer and a tear traces down my face. Sam takes me to sit on the stairs that lead to the apartment. I wipe my eyes and mutter something about acting like a baby.

"Don't be ridiculous," says Sam . "You're the strongest person I've ever known."

"Yeah, right." Tears gather at my eyelids. I blink them back.

"You are," Sam insists. "Remember when you thought Will was hitting me?"

"One of my finer moments."

"Stop it," she says. "The point is, you stood strong where not one friend in a thousand would have."

I make a grunting sound she can interpret however she wants.

"I've know you since you were little, and I'm so proud of who you've become." She leans in. "And you've done it all with one parent. Trust me; I know how hard that is."

I guess she does. Her dad didn't find Sylvia for

almost four years after Sam's mom was killed. And then it hits me: if Ma is the one who got the toxin, and if she dies, I will have no one.

I cover my face with my hands. Hot tears push right through my lids, even though they're shut tight.

Sam hugs me, says more stuff about how everything's going to be okay.

"I know," I say, swallowing hard. I wipe my eyes with the backs of my hands. Because that's so mature-looking. "It's just … I couldn't handle losing my mom, okay?"

"Hey, no one is dying here," says Sam.

"I love her," I say. "I mean, I joke about her and roll my eyes, but if anything were to happen…."

Chrétien eyes us from a few feet away, looking super distressed. He walks over and kneels so his eyes are on the same level as mine. "*Mademoiselle,*" he says, "upon my honor and upon the souls of my wife and child, I will die before I will allow any harm to come to your family."

I know, now, what a vow like this means coming from Chrétien.

"Ma and the aunties—they're all I have," I whisper softly.

"No," says Sam. "If there's one thing I've know, it's that family is more than just blood ties."

"Indeed, *Mademoiselle,*" adds Chrétien, "you are not alone."

I look from Sam's face to Chrétien's and back again.

Slowly I nod. I repeat the words. "I'm not alone."

After this, time feels like it's rushing past until we have less than three hours before Fritz's deadline. I sit by Ma's side, refilling her mug of herb tea and those of her sisters. They tell me I am a good daughter, which only makes it harder to not cry. I take to walking up and down the stairs because it is too hard to be still and impossible to be anywhere but here at the bakery, waiting.

I mutter, "Where is the bastard?" for the fifth or sixth time, when we hear a car pulling up in back by the cat kennels. I don't know what I was expecting, but there is something so ordinary in the sound of tires crunching through our backyard gravel. Bad guy cars shouldn't sound ordinary. They should sound ominous. Evil. I clench my hands into fists.

There's a knock at the door.

Chapter Twenty-Five

THE WRONG JOURNAL

Sir Walter answers the knock at the door.

The motion detector lights shine on not one, but *two* bad guys, neither of whom looks like the middle-aged brother of Hans and Franz. They're too young, for one thing. Then I recognize them.

"Hansel," says Sir Walter, doing one of his little bows. "And Georg." Another bow.

"Step back from the door," says Hansel. "You will remain at all times no less than seven meters distant from both of us."

"That'll be hard, considering the room's only fifteen by eighteen feet," mutters Ma. She came downstairs awhile back, but she made the aunties stay upstairs. She tried to make me go upstairs, too. Yeah. Right.

Apparently Hansel and Gretel aren't great judges of distance; they don't object when they see the room. Our group shuffles back to the small prep table against the wall that backs into the café. The Brothers Blond walk inside the bakery, where they hug the back exit.

Gretel opens a tablet screen and Hansel explains what's going to happen.

"Doctor Gottlieb will address you via this monitor."

Gretel walks toward us, setting the tablet up on the central work station so that the monitor faces us.

"That's how Helmann communicated with Franz and Fritz," Sam whispers to me.

"No whisperings," says Hansel. "Should my brother or I feel ourselves in danger, we will disappear." Hansel holds up a single syringe. "If what Uncle Fritz tells us is true, you don't want us to disappear."

"Please," says Sir Walter, addressing Hansel. "Allow us to administer the antidote."

Fritz's face, overlarge, appears on the monitor screen. "Not yet, not yet. Greetings de Rochefort. I suppose I should call you *cousin*, but we've never really been close, have we?" He smiles and I swear I want to punch the monitor.

"The journal?" asks Fritz. "You have it?"

Sir Walter takes it from his jacket, slowly, holding it up so Fritz can see it.

"Good, good," says Fritz.

"Give us the anti-serum," says Sir Walter.

225

"In good time," says Fritz. "The antidote won't do you any good until you know who it's for, anyway."

I scowl, but I force myself to keep my mouth shut. Getting that antidote is the only thing that matters right now. I won't make it worse by opening my big mouth.

"Set the book on the table beside the monitor," says Hansel, evidently the one in charge between him and Gretel. He acted the same way back in Sir Walter's farmhouse.

"Do as he instructs you," Fritz says. "Slowly. No sudden moves or the Angels fly away." He smiles at his stupid little joke.

I roll my eyes. I don't care if he sees it. Then I realize I should care. Come on, Gwyn!

Sir Walter walks to the table and sets the book down. "The antidote, please," he says. His voice is as calm as if he is asking a waiter for the check.

But Fritz shakes his head. "First things first, cousin. Back away so that Georg can examine the document to see if it meets my approval."

It doesn't look to me like Georg is packing any lab equipment. I wonder how he's planning to scrape off old Helmann cells or whatever he's supposed to do. Georg walks to the table and back super fast, his eyes trained on Sir Walter. He's obviously nervous about getting close to him. It's me he should be nervous about. I'm mentally reviewing every self-defense move I know.

Georg takes the journal to where Hansel waits at

the back door. For a split-second, it looks to me like we've done this all wrong. Like they're about to leave without giving us the serum or even telling us who needs it. But they don't try to run. They bend over the journal.

"Well?" demands Fritz. Ridiculously, he says it to us, because he can't see the two brothers with the monitor pointed our direction.

"They're verifying the journal is genuine," says Sir Walter, his voice calm and assured.

I wish I felt half that calm. My stomach is twisting over on itself like a pretzel.

"Boys?" asks Fritz. You can tell he's irritated they haven't said anything yet.

"There seems to be a problem, Uncle Fritz," says Hansel. "This is not the journal you are looking for."

"What do you mean?" demands Mickie. "Of course it's Helmann's journal. Full of every spiteful little thing he ever did to you and your siblings." She practically spits the words out and I sort of love her right now.

"It looks genuine," says Hansel, "but it is not the correct one. Have you brought the other one, Mr. de Rochefort?"

"That's *Sir* Mr. de Rochefort to you," I snap.

Everyone ignores me.

"Cousin?" demands Fritz. "Are you playing games with me? I warned you. A life is at stake. Consider carefully what you are doing."

My heart starts racing. I shouldn't have taunted

him. Nothing matters but making him happy enough to give us that antidote.

"I brought what you asked for," says Sir Walter. There's a dangerous edge to his voice.

"No," says Hansel. "I overheard you and Pfeffer speaking of another journal. A second one. When you were speaking mind-to-mind, I heard you."

Pfeffer nearly chokes as he responds. "But that's impossible. You don't 'hear' anything when you're invisible. I tested you for it. All of you. Only Martina has that gift."

Hansel's cheeks turn pink. "You tested us. It does not follow we cooperated in responding to your questions."

Pfeffer and Mickie swear at the same time.

"You brought me the wrong journal?" Fritz shouts the question. "I warned you, de Rochefort! Hansel, Georg: you will depart. Leave the monitor in place, my nephews. I want to see the look on my cousin's face when the Asian woman perishes."

Hansel and Georg vanish from sight, the space where they stood rippling slightly.

"No!" I cry out. My hands fly to my mouth. This can't be happening.

Chapter Twenty-Six

LIKED HIS SCHNAPPS

"Wait!" cries Chrétien. In his hand, he holds the other journal. He lifts it for Fritz to see. "Here. We have what you want."

"No, Chrétien!" cries Mickie.

Pfeffer, at her side, holds her back. "It's not worth it," he murmurs to Mickie. "The price of a human life is too high a price to pay."

Mickie shakes her head. Then she nods once. Twice.

Fritz allows one side of his mouth to curve into a smile. "Very smart. Very wise, indeed. Hansel, Georg, please come back."

Hansel and Georg solidify, one after the other, on the far side of the room.

From the monitor on the table where I've

229

scooped ten thousand cookies alongside my mom, Fritz speaks slowly and carefully.

"Let's try this again, shall we? This had better be the right journal, this time."

Sir Walter shrugs. "I had no way of knowing which one you wanted."

"Hmm," replies Fritz. "And you thought to keep one for yourself. How selfish of you. Georg? Is it genuine?"

Georg is flipping through the pages. "It appears to be the one missing from Aunt Helga's laboratory," he says. "The dates are right."

My heart sinks. They knew about the two journals all along. At least, they knew they wanted the one Sam stole from Helga's lab at UC Merced.

"Test its authenticity," Fritz orders.

Georg addresses us. "We have to disappear to test the journal. I swear we will return."

"You can't leave!" I cry out. "We've only got two hours!"

"We're not leaving, only vanishing," he says. "We'll be right here, conducting the examination. It should take only a minute. Less, maybe."

And they disappear.

"What are they doing?" I demand, turning to Pfeffer, to Sir Walter.

The two men shrug, both as clueless as I am.

I turn to the monitor. "Hansel's coming back with the antidote, isn't he?" I'm begging Fritz.

"I should think he's nearly done, my dear," Fritz

says to me. "You see, my friends, Georg has a remarkable gift. He has a sense of smell, when in chameleon form, which is quite unparalleled."

At Sam's side, Will snorts. I don't know what's funny here. My skin crawls the way he says, "*my dear*" and "*my friends*," but I try not to let it show. I remind myself. I'll do anything for the antidote.

Georg ripples back solid, alone. "It smells of Dr. Helmann," he says, addressing Fritz, "but it also smells strongly of mint and something else—alcohol, perhaps. I don't know what to think, Uncle."

Fritz grins. "Schnapps," he says. "Father liked his Schnapps. Helga scolded him once for spilling some on his journals. Well done, Georg, my boy! Well done." Fritz changes his tone as he addresses Sir Walter and the rest of us. "This time, I believe you have supplied what I requested for our little trade. Hansel, time is running out for *Bridget Li*. You may deliver the antidote." He smiles wickedly. "Did you guess correctly, any of you?"

I feel it again, that sensation that my lungs are being crushed. I suck against the feeling, drawing in air, refusing to let Fritz see my fear. Of course he would pick her. Fritz was the one who *liked* hurting kittens. He would strike Pfeffer and Sir Walter hardest if he struck me hardest. Which meant choosing my mother.

Hansel comes solid. He glances at Gretel and gives him a tiny nod. Gretel nods back. What is that about? I don't have time to worry about their nonverbals, though. Hansel holds the serum in an outstretched hand.

My entire focus shifts there, my world in the palm of his hand.

"I won't come any closer to the rest of you chameleons," says Hansel. "If any of you disappear, so will I, along with the serum. Send one of the visibles over here to get it."

"Visibles?" mutters Will.

"Non-ripplers," says Mick. "I'll go."

"No," I say, striding boldly forward. This is my bakery, my mom, my responsibility.

Halfway across the room, something sort of itches at the edge of my consciousness. Why doesn't Hansel just set down the serum and ripple away? I close the distance. It doesn't matter *why* he won't. He said I had to walk over. Fine. They make the rules; I do whatever it takes.

"Hand it over," I say, my hand outstretched before the pair of bleach-heads.

One second, I am standing with my hand outstretched, a look of determination on my face. The next second, Georg grabs me and pins me with one arm.

Chapter Twenty-Seven

MONOLOGUE-ING

As Georg grabs me, Hansel moves with lightning speed to the monitor, flipping it around. Then Hansel ripples and Georg, one hand securing me, one hand holding the journal, speaks to my friends.

"Don't move or I disappear with her. I don't want to harm her. Cooperate and I'll release her in a moment, along with the antidote."

"What do you want?" asks Sir Walter.

"Give me the antidote!" I scream.

At the same moment, Fritz shouts from the monitor, "Get out of there, you fools. Do you know how dangerous de Rochefort is?"

I can see the fear in Fritz's eyes.

Good, I think. You'd *better* be afraid.

"Uncle Fritz, there's been a change of plans," says

233

Georg. "Hansel and I will be keeping the journal for ourselves. We appreciate all you've done for us, but we don't want to live under your control any more than we wanted to live under Pfeffer's control."

He's *monologue*-ing. He's freaking bad guy *monologue*-ing. At a time like this! With my mother's life at stake!

I shout in the direction of Hansel, "Give me the serum—*now!*"

Georg twists my arm more firmly. "Please, another moment," he says to me. He turns to speak to Fritz again. "My brother and I have procured enough of the enzyme from your lab to keep ourselves healthy for months. And by the time we run out, we'll have figured out how to make more. Or one of our other siblings will do so."

My arm is hurting where Georg has it twisted back. But I can still use some of my self defense moves. I can Sandra Bullock the heck out of his *sternum, instep, nose* and *groin*. Make Gretel *S-I-N-G*. I'm getting myself in position when I notice the *crème brulée* torch right next to my free hand.

Gretel, who is now engaging Fritz in a shouting match about civil rights, has set the journal down right in front of me to gesticulate more effectively.

His grip on me loosens slightly and I slip free, grabbing the journal and the mini flame thrower. I would have liked to have hit him, but this isn't about what I would like. It's about what I have to do. It's about what I can't live without.

"Give me the serum!" I shout, as loud as I can, "or I burn the journal!"

I power the *crème brulée* torch on high.

Out of the corner of my eye, I see Chrétien ripple invisible. But my focus is on Hansel, who has just come solid. His hand, which had held the antidote, is empty.

Why is his hand empty? What happened to the antidote?

I scream. "Where is—"

But something interrupts me. The something is Chrétien, who appears three feet away, running for all he's worth, his arms flung wide. I can see what he's planning—to grab me. And then things go horribly, horribly wrong. As Chrétien grabs me, he jostles the journal toward the flame thrower. The ancient pages ignite at once and, on impulse, I release the flaming book just as Chrétien ripples both of us to invisibility.

No! I cry. *The journal!*

It's my leverage.

And I dropped it.

And it's burning.

No! I cry again.

I hear Chrétien mutter a horrified, *Mon Dieu!*

He releases me, leaving me invisibly trapped in nothingness, and now things happen fast and thick. Chrétien comes solid, reaching for the flaming book. Seeing Chrétien come solid, Hansel vanishes. I can't move. The journal flares in Chrétien's hands. Instinctively, he casts it away, crying out in pain.

Georg runs to grab the book, but he stops in his tracks, seeing Chrétien coming at him all *Hulk! Smash!*

Chrétien! I cry out. *The serum!*

But he's still trying to rescue the burning journal. I can see it's no use. The book is destroyed beyond all legibility. The leather cover is all that's left now.

We have nothing to offer, nothing to trade.

Invisible, I howl in frustration.

Hansel comes solid long enough to scream, "Vanish!" to his brother. Chrétien follows both of them into invisibility.

And then it gets noisy. Really noisy. Inside my head.

I'm shouting to Chrétien that my mother is going to die. Chrétien is telling me he's searching for Hansel. And I hear them, the blond brothers, speaking to one another.

The journal is lost, Georg is saying. *Give them the serum and let us depart.*

Hansel answers, *I don't have it.*

What? I scream it along with Georg.

I must have let it slip in the moment I saw the girl attacking, says Hansel.

You let go of it? demands Georg.

It's gone, says Hansel. *Let's go.*

We have to tell them, says Georg.

We owe them nothing, says Hansel. *I'm leaving. I'll see you at the rendezvous.*

In an instant, it's silent. Except for one voice.

Gwyn?

It's Chrétien.

Please, Mademoiselle *Gwyn*, he says. *I cannot discover you. Where are you?*

I say nothing.

I am uncertain where I left you when I fled, says Chrétien. *Please. Can you hear me?*

I could answer. I could tell him that I am poised right over the cracked linoleum tile that Ma is always saying we need to replace. That I am standing beside the table that had to be custom built inside the bakery because Ma insisted the ones in the restaurant supply warehouse were too small. That I am three feet from the stairs leading to the apartment my mother and I have shared, just us together, no aunties, no dinners, just me and Ma.

I could answer Chrétien, but I don't. What does it matter?

My mother is going to die and it's my fault and there is nothing I can do to save her.

Chapter Twenty-Eight

IT'S MY FAULT

I hear Sir Walter. I hear Sam. I see Will's ridiculous writing.

All of them, I ignore.

Finally, they stop calling for me and simply talk among themselves.

"She needs some time by herself," says Sam.

"She needs to grow a pair," says Mickie.

"Mick," says Will. "Enough."

She hangs her head and mutters an apology. I can tell she's worried.

Chrétien is retracing his steps where he grabbed me, calling my name softly inside my head.

"Sir Walter," says Will. "You're good at finding stuff. Even small stuff, like that bullet you took out of me, right?"

"Ah," says Sir Walter. "Of course. I shall seek her out."

I watch as he ripples and disappears.

Pfeffer is bringing Ma and the aunties back down to the bakery. My heart wrenches when I see my mother. She doesn't look good.

Sir Walter? I call out. Because, all of the sudden, I don't want to be invisible any more. I want my mom.

Before I can repeat the call, he arrives, finding me, and I feel my skin coming back into solid reality.

I run into my mother's arms. The aunties cluck and mumble about demons and curses.

"It's my fault, Ma," I say. "I'm so sorry. I'm so, so sorry."

My mother pulls back from the hug and grabs me squarely by the shoulders. "You listen to me, Gwyneth Li," she says, her voice weak. "This is not your fault. Dr. Pfeffer has explained what happened. That I got the deadly injection. But *you* were not the one pulling the plunger on that syringe. This is *not* your fault."

She gives me a small shake with those last three words. And I guess there must be something to that old saying about someone knocking some sense into you, because I realize something incredible.

"*Sir Walter!*" I say, hope flaring inside me. "You can find things. Small things. When they're invisible." I'm so excited I can hardly form sentences. "Find the syringe! With the antidote!"

Sir Walter's eyes close and he shakes his head. "Of course," he says as he melts into thin air.

As soon as Sir Walter vanishes, Pfeffer speaks solemnly to my mother. "We should ripple you to insubstantiality. It will halt the spread of the toxin. I should have thought of this earlier."

Another spark of hope ignites inside me, and I take my mom's hand, nodding.

"Oh, no," she says, shaking her head.

"Ma! Don't be stupid," I say. "You're going to be invisible and you're going to say thank you and you're going to like it."

My mom stares at me for a minute and my aunties murmur about ungrateful daughters, and I am pretty sure I'm about to have every bad word in the Mandarin dialect aimed my direction by my dying mother.

But then she un-knits those dark eyebrows and turns to Chrétien. "Would you be so kind as to take me to safety? My daughter speaks highly of your skills."

I make a choking, laughing noise. I have spoken highly of many things pertaining to Chrétien, but his rippling skills would not be one of them.

A moment later, Ma is gone and Chrétien is back.

And we wait. Again.

There is no guarantee Sir Walter, even with his ability to sense small items, is going to locate the antidote. I pace, wearing a track around the work table in the bakery, jogging up and down the stairs.

After an hour or so, Will decides to help Sir Walter look. "It's better than standing here doing nothing."

I watch, jealous, as the air where he stood ripples and settles.

Chrétien has been following me with his eyes the whole time and saying nothing. But now he breaks off from this fascinating pursuit to help Will and Sir Walter.

My legs start turning to jelly after about two hours of non-stop motion, and I sink onto the second stair tread from the bottom, sighing heavily. Sam comes to sit with me.

"It's my fault," I say. "I torched the journal."

"Oh, Gwyn, not you, too." She shakes her head.

"What do you mean, not me, too?"

"Chrétien kept saying the same thing," she says. "How it's his fault. But it's not. It's no one's fault."

"It's Fritz's fault."

Sam nods. "Yes. Yes, it is."

My voice drops to a whisper. "I don't know how I'll live with myself if ..."

Sam takes my hand and squeezes it hard.

Oh, dear God. She knows. She knows what I'm feeling. I bury my head in her shoulder. And Chrétien. He knows, too. I finally understand how foolish I've been with all of my chasing and cheering up and, just, everything. There are some things you don't ever bounce back from. I weep silently on the shoulder of my best friend.

An hour later, I hear Chrétien's voice, clear and loud, from inside my head: *We have discovered it!*

Will reappears in front of me and Sam, talking a mile a minute. "Hansel didn't just 'let it slip,'" he says. "Oh, no, that would have been too easy. No, when Hansel saw Gwyn accidentally set fire to Helmann's *Journal of Secret*, Hansel *flung* that syringe through the bakery wall, and it landed outside in Woody Allen's cat kennel."

"Stop talking and get my mom!" I shout.

A few minutes later, when Chrétien has brought Ma back, Dr. Pfeffer administers the antidote. Ma doesn't look good, and she's not talking at all. Pfeffer monitors her with something he must have stolen from Dr. Yang's office down the street. Well, it's the middle of the night and no one's going to miss it.

An hour passes, during which time I hold my mom's hand and stare at her closed eyes. Another hour passes and Ma speaks.

The first thing she asks, when she starts talking again, is how Woody Allen is doing. Not, *Gwyn, my darling, did you sit here with me all this time?* But, *Is Woody Allen recovering from having that invisible syringe thrown at him?*

So, basically, the Li family is back to normal.

Chapter Twenty-Nine

YOU DON'T GO BACK TO THE BAT CAVE

"That's it," I say to Sam, shaking my head. "The world is officially coming to an end."

After sleeping for eight hours straight, Ma has just gotten up and announced she is going to make dinner. Without any help. The aunties flew back to LA, so there isn't anyone to help anyway.

"But Ma doesn't know how to make dinner," I say, after she goes downstairs.

Sam shrugs. "It is just possible your mom knows how to do things you don't know she knows how to do."

I grunt. "We should have asked Will to make pizza." Seriously. Because who knows what my mom is going to try and feed us. Unfortunately, Will went back to his house with Mickie awhile ago.

Chrétien and Pfeffer and Sir Walter stayed here to discuss Important Things, although Chrétien has barely opened his mouth the entire time. He just stares at the table like the wood grain is encoded with the Secrets of the Universe or something. Occasionally, he runs a thumb around and around a stain from a coffee mug. Once, he answers a question that Sir Walter directs to him.

"What was it Martina told you about never speaking of the pass phrase?" asks Sir Walter.

"She gave me to understand that the sleepers fear falling once more under the sway of others. They divined, somehow, that a phrase exists which exerts control over them. They do not know what it is. They vowed not to speak of it to Fritz, in the hope he knew not of its existence."

"He knows," says Pfeffer. "I can confirm that he sought to discover Helmann's password while I still worked at Geneses. Franz was furious with him for trying."

"But Fritz saw the journal go up in flames," I say. "So we should be in the clear, right?"

Chrétien runs a finger around, around, around the coffee stain.

"Indeed," says Sir Walter. "As you saw, he bears me no love, but I believe he will concentrate his efforts upon locating Hansel and Georg."

"Or upon saving Geneses Corporation from ruin," says Pfeffer.

At this point, Ma calls all of us down to dinner,

and we gather around the oversized prep-table in the bakery kitchen. I am in shock when I see stir-fry veggies and potstickers and rice. It all smells delicious.

"Honestly," I whisper to Sam, "this is very disturbing."

Just then, Pfeffer gets a text message from Mickie, who must have bought a new phone in the last eight hours. I have given up trying to decide if they are together or not. But maybe they are, because Pfeffer looks up and tells us Will and Mickie invited him over for a meal, too. He's looking all worried abut offending my mom, so I let him off the hook.

"There might actually be enough food for the rest of us if you would just leave, already," I say.

This earns me a smattering of Chinese from Ma, all about hospitality and my shortcomings as a daughter.

Sir Walter steps into the gap, gracefully complimenting Ma on the excellence of her food. He and my mom then discuss the regional cuisines of China, and she points out that what she made is very Americanized, actually.

Across from us, Chrétien picks at his food, too polite to avoid eating altogether, but his heart's not in it. It might be time to reboot Operation Cheer Chrétien Up, after all.

"I shall, of course, be most anxious to consult you as to the best markets when it comes time to stock my own kitchen," says Sir Walter.

"Sir Walter is staying for awhile," Ma tells me.

"He's never seen Yosemite."

"Really?" I ask. I mean, I know people exist who haven't seen Yosemite. But I would have thought Sir Walter might have managed it once in his six centuries.

"He'll be staying in the Oak Street rental," Ma tells me.

"He will?" I ask.

Sir Walter smiles. "Your dear mother insisted."

"We owe him *both* our lives," she says quietly. "The least I can do is offer him a place to stay."

"For free?" I ask my mom.

"Don't be rude, Gwyn," says Ma.

"For free?" I ask Sir Walter.

He smiles. "She would have it no other way."

I ready myself for another tongue-lashing, but it never comes.

I turn to Sam and mouth the words, *That's not my mom. Who is she?*

Sam rolls her eyes and ignores me.

Sir Walter and Ma have moved on to a discussion of where to buy clothes and a trustworthy frying pan.

"Regrettably," says Sir Walter, "I do not foresee the opportunity to return to retrieve my simple belongings in Carcassonne any time soon."

He's got a point: you don't go back to the Bat Cave once the Joker knows how to get in.

Chrétien, sitting across from me, looks like he's trying to read a secret message in the potsticker sauce. He frowns and his eyes pinch shut for a brief moment. Then he sets his napkin on the table, rises, bows to my mother, and begs leave to be excused. Ma, overwhelmed by the abundance of polite language, nods.

Chrétien crosses out of the room without speaking to anyone else. Sir Walter looks grave as he watches his son depart.

"Do you know what's wrong with Chrétien?" I whisper to Sam.

She shrugs like she's not sure.

I frown. Chrétien's been off all day. He's barely made eye contact with me, which last week wouldn't have been a big deal, but I thought things were changing between us, lately. I mean, not in the direction I once hoped, but since he told me all those stories, it seemed like maybe we'd connected in a new way.

Sir Walter scratches away at his goatee like he can make it purr. Then he breathes out heavily and asks to be excused as well. Maybe to keep Chrétien company.

And now it's just the three of us: me, Sam, and Ma.

"Well," says Ma, with a big sigh, "I'm all for them sticking around to keep an eye on Las Abuelitas, but I have to admit, I always feel like I don't know which fork to use around those two."

Sam laughs. "It gets easier."

I let Sam and my mom carry the conversation without me. Finally, Ma announces she's going to sleep some more and tells me to do the dishes.

"Sure thing," I say.

I take the first load of dishes to the sink and start rinsing.

Sam brings me the rest of the dishes, and I spray away. I'm still worried about Chrétien. I scan back through the dinner conversation, in case I made some atrocious Gwyn-comment that might account for his getting up and leaving. But for once, I don't think I said anything offensive.

"I think those dishes are good," Sam says.

I look down at the plates in the sink. Not a spot of food to be seen. I sigh and start loading our industrial dishwasher.

"What is it?" she asks me.

"Chrétien. He hasn't said a word to me all day. I'm worried about him."

Sam's mouth pulls to one side. It's her anxious face.

"And you are, too," I say. "What's going on with him?"

"I don't know for sure. I overheard him and Sir Walter earlier, talking about leaving things or leaving the past or something like that, but they stopped talking when I walked in the room."

Leaving things.

Things like … his wife's golden slipper? I feel a flush of heat. It begins at my chest and works up my neck and onto my face. I swing around the dishwasher, locking it down, my hair a curtain hiding my face from Sam.

What have I done? What was I thinking?

"I think it was hard on him, watching your mom getting sick," says Sam. "You know, because of how he lost his wife and his daughter to sickness."

I nod.

"I'm sure he'll be back to normal soon," says Sam. "Happy as ever."

I punch the button and the dishwasher groans into action.

What have I done? And why did I think the decision was mine to make in the first place? It would have been so easy to grab that slipper—the last thing he had to remember her by. I grip the edge of the sink. What was I thinking?

"Hey," says Sam. "Are you okay?"

"Oh, Sam ..." I shake my head. The fact that I'm embarrassed to tell her confirms for me I did a very, very wrong thing. But I have to tell someone. I take a short breath and let it spill out. "I left the shoe in France," I say, watching the water swirl down the drain and wishing I could swirl down after it myself.

"Your new red shoes?" She gives me a little side hug. "What do you want to bet you can get another pair when you go back to collect your passport and legally exit France?"

"Not *my* shoes," I say. "*The* shoe. Cinderella's slipper of gold."

"Oh," says Sam. "*That* shoe."

"Yes," I say. "*That* shoe. And Chrétien will never forgive me when he finds out."

"Gwyn." Sam wraps an arm around my shoulder.

"Can you say, 'over-reacting'?"

I shake my head. "I'm not over-reacting. You said he was talking to Sir Walter about leaving stuff behind."

"Hmm," says Sam. "Yeah. I guess he must have been talking about the slipper. I mean, the diary was already pretty much off the table. Oh, poor Chrétien."

I feel tears burning behind my eyes and blink them back. "It's my fault for not grabbing it when I had the chance."

"Your fault? How can you say that? Of course it's not your fault. It's not like you did it on purpose."

I don't say anything. I just concentrate on not crying.

"Are you worried he'll think you did it on purpose? You shouldn't. I don't think his mind operates that way."

"Oh, Sam—" I can't talk. I want to disappear. My face heats up again until I'm sure I'm beet red.

"Gwyn? What are you not telling me?" Her eyes narrow as she figures it out. "Oh, no. You thought about going back for it, didn't you? But you didn't say anything. Um, Gwyn? You want to tell me I'm wrong here?"

"I thought … I thought maybe if he left all of that behind, it would help," I say softly.

"Oh, Gwyn." Her voice is soft, but I can hear the accusation.

"I know. It wasn't my decision to make. I can see that *now*."

"You have to tell him. You have to apologize."

"I know." She's right. I owe him that apology. "He'll hate me once he hears what I did."

"Hate is a pretty strong word, Gwyn."

I don't think it's too strong.

"Maybe he was ready to let it go, anyway," says Sam. "If the slipper was left behind in the farmhouse, he wasn't exactly keeping it close, was he?"

"That was my fault, too," I say. "He used to keep it safe at the Well of Juno, but after he showed me, we brought it back to the cottage. I was going to show it to you. Only, Hansel and Georg got there before I had a chance."

"Hmm...." Sam stares down at the floor.

"I don't think I can bear it if he hates me," I say.

"He won't hate you, Gwynnie. He's not like that."

"It was the last thing he had to remind him of Marie-Anne," I say.

Sam shrugs. "Things are over-rated."

"How can you say that? What was the one thing you wanted from your house when it was on fire?"

She stares at me. "Sylvia and Chrétien to be okay?"

"No," I say. "You had Chrétien go back and grab your mom's painting of Yosemite. Remember?"

She frowns and nods. "Yeah. I see what you mean."

"The picture is all you have left of your mom," I say. "And Marie-Anne's shoe was all Chrétien had left of his wife."

"I love my mom's painting," Sam says, "and if it was stolen tomorrow, I'm not going to lie, I would be heartbroken."

I moan.

"I would be heartbroken," Sam repeats, "but I would survive."

If she's trying to make me feel better, it's not working. I think about the way Chrétien stared at the coffee mug stain. About the way he avoided looking at me. I think about the stories he told me. How much he loved them, Marie-Anne and Madeleine. I shake my head.

"I think Chrétien's different," I say.

"Well," replies Sam, "there's one way you could find out."

"There is?"

"When you apologize, ask him what the slipper meant to him."

"I could no more ask him that than I could *fly*," I say.

"Or turn invisible," says Sam. "Or hear voices in your head. Or have conversations with the people whose voices you hear."

"Shut up," I say. "That's not fair."

Sam laughs. Soft. Poignant. "Oh, Gwyn. Who ever said life is fair?"

I sigh heavily. A single tear slides down one side of my face. Sam sees it and wipes it dry.

"You've got it bad for him, don't you?"

I nod. More tears join the first one.

252

"What if he never forgives me?"

"I think he'll forgive you. Someday. He's really, *really* into forgiveness. Although, it might take awhile. Give him time, Gwyn."

"In case it escaped your notice, I don't have an infinity of years waiting in my back pocket like you guys."

Sam takes my hand, giving it a quick squeeze.

"Just one more reason 'we' can't ever be an 'us,'" I say. "Chrétien and I are incompatible on a genetic level."

Sam doesn't argue this point, and I guess it's because there's really no getting around the fact that I will never be a rippler, and Chrétien probably ought to date someone who's going to be around a few centuries.

Neither of us says anything for several minutes. At last Sam tells me she promised Will she'd stop by after dinner. "You going to be okay?" she asks.

"I'll be fine," I say. "You know me."

"Promise me you'll talk to Chrétien," she says.

"I promise I'll apologize," I say. I don't make any promises about asking him what the golden slipper meant to him.

Chapter Thirty

LIKE AN ACCUSATION

After Sam goes, I do something I haven't done for over a year. When Ma's center work table was being built, I discovered I could sit on the bottom "shelf" where Ma stores the fifty pound bags of powdered sugar and the twenty-six inch sheet pans. It's a perfect place to hide out and take stock. I reach underneath and shove one of the heavy sacks over a few inches. Then I grab all six sheet pans and set them on top of the table. When I'm done, there's just enough room for Gwyn, and I crawl in.

Using the back of my hand, I knock a dent in the top of the sugar sack for my neck to rest on, and then I sink back against the bag. From under here, I can see samples of my handwriting. Messier on days I came here to blow off steam, tidy and precise on days I came here to think things through.

I'm not sure which kind of day today is.

I reach under one of the two by four supports and feel around for my Sharpie. Ma used to wonder where all the Sharpies went when we first moved here. I used to shrug like I had no clue. It's been so long now I don't know if this one will write. I pop the top off and draw a curving arc from a list of boys I liked to a letter I wrote my dad last Father's Day. I guess it hasn't been quite a year since the last time I felt the need to crawl in here. The pen works just fine. You've got to love a pen that can write upside down after eight months.

I'm not here to blow off steam today. So, why am I here?

I write the question in big flowy letters covering the letter to my dad.

Why Is Gwyn Here?

It's a good question. Why am I here?

I'm not sure.

My hand moves and another question snakes across the previous lists and rants in dark, black Sharpie.

Who Is Gwyn, Anyway?

I stare at the new question. Who am I? I think about the attributes I rattled off the other day for Sam—the ones comprising my Gwynitude.

Confident.

Independent.

Boy magnet.

255

I substitute that last one for the one about naps in warm places. The napping quip was me making a joke, and this is a serious time.

Never serious, I write. I chew on the end of the pen for a minute and then raise it to a clean space.

Selfish.

Competitive.

Life of the party.

Self-absorbed. I almost put a line through that one, because it sounds like "selfish," but then I decide it is different from "selfish" and that it is also very true if me.

And then, because I'm staring right at a list of boys I've left in my wake, I come up with two more. *Manipulative*, I write. And then, beside it: *Heart-breaker.* I doodle a heart, cracked into two halves, jagged edges, messy.

Reading through the list, I am struck by something. If someone described a person like this to me, I would probably make a snarky comment about how the person sounds *very* controlling—a total control freak—and what are they compensating for, anyway?

Ouch.

Close to home, much? What was I trying to do when I chose to leave Chrétien's shoe behind? I was trying to control things. To run his life for him.

I shut my eyes so I don't have to look at what I've written. But I see a word.

Selfish.

And then, beside it, the laundry list of related attributes flash across my brain.

Manipulative.

Self-absorbed.

Heart-breaker.

"Stop it," I mutter to myself. "Gwyns are the life of the party. Gwyns are confident."

It's true. I am those things.

But the other stuff is true, too. And together, they make up a picture of someone I don't like. Who would? Not Chrétien; that's for sure. I think about all the different ways I've pursued him this past two months since we met. First I wanted him as a sort of new, flashy accessory: *boy-bling*. Then, when he didn't immediately fall at my feet, I wanted him because he presented a challenge.

Later, maybe just before I got kidnapped, I started actually liking him for his own sake and not for mine. Then I found out about his past and things shifted inside me. But even though I switched from "chase Chrétien" mode to "cheer Chrétien up" mode, I didn't completely give up making him mine. And I sure wasn't planning on letting him go when I decided he'd be better off never seeing that slipper again.

I look at the list of old boyfriends again. This time, it reads like an accusation. I never really cared about any of them. I just cared about how they made me feel less alone. A tear rolls down my face and slides off at my jaw line, making a tiny *tap* when it hits the powdered sugar bag behind my head.

257

It's time for me to let Chrétien go. He deserves the chance to heal. On his own terms and at his own pace. The best way for me to make sure that happens is to step out of his life before I do any more damage.

But first, that apology. Not so he can forgive me—I don't deserve that any more than I deserve his friendship. But I will apologize. Because even if I don't deserve anything, he does. He deserves to know the truth about me.

Chapter Thirty-One

UNSPEAKABLY AWKWARD

The sun is going to set soon in Las Abuelitas, so I decide to look outside first. I find Sir Walter across the street from the bakery, but no Chrétien. Sir Walter is smoking one of his smelly French cigarettes. I cross the street to speak with him.

"Do you know where Chrétien went?" I ask. "I have to talk to him."

"Yes, I know where he can be found," says Sir Walter. "He will be most delighted, I think, to see you."

Yeah. Sure he will. Not. But that doesn't matter. It is time to put on my big girl pull-ups and do this thing.

"Where is he?" I ask.

"At the hot spring. How is it called ... *Belle*

259

Froide?"

"Wrong language," I say. "Assuming you mean Bella Fria." It's the only hot spring I know of in this area.

"Ah, yes, how foolish of me."

"Do you know when he'll be back?" I ask. It's a ninety minute hike, one way, from the greater Las Abuelitas metropolitan area.

"I do not," says Sir Walter.

I frown and cross my arms. I don't want to be gone from Ma (just in case) for a whole three hours plus the time it takes to apologize. Figures I would get my brave on when I can't put it to any use.

"*Mademoiselle,*" says Sir Walter, "Chrétien traveled invisibly so as to arrive with less delay. Might I offer to transport you thither, to lessen the time you are apart from your dear mother?"

I hesitate. "I don't want to be a bother."

"It is no bother. I can have you there very swiftly. It is a good place for a friend of chameleons to visit."

"Yeah," I say. "Sam told me about the gold and tobiasite stuff."

"May I take you as well?"

"Sure," I say. A few minutes later, we vanish from inside the bakery where no one can freak out seeing it happen. And a few minutes after that, we arrive at the spring.

When we get there, Chrétien's visible. I take that as a good sign.

As soon as we come solid, Chrétien turns to me, a

polite if strained smile on his face. Sir Walter does a little goodbye bow and vanishes. Which means I'm going to have to ask Chrétien for a ride home, unless I want to hike back.

I sit down across from him on a little granite boulder. Steam from the spring hits my face. My courage seems to have forgotten to come solid with me. But this isn't about how I feel.

"So, here's the thing," I say, determined to start so I can't chicken out. "I made you go with me that time I wanted jeans, and that made you forget about your wife's diary, and that made Fritz find it and steal it. And I'm really sorry. For making you get stupid jeans with me and lose the diary." I take a breath and get ready to apologize for the shoe—the thing that's made him so depressed all day.

"Unfortunately, I did something worse. Like, a lot worse. When we saw Hansel and Gretel—sorry, Georg—enter the farmhouse, I thought of your wife's golden slipper right away. And I totally could have asked Sam to come solid with me so that we could snatch it for you when the two sleeper dudes were preoccupied with my phone. But I didn't." I take a really deep breath. "I wanted ... I hoped ... I thought that maybe if you didn't have anything of hers left, it would make you more interested in ... well, in other ... *things* ... in the here and now."

This is unspeakably awkward. Only my belief that Chrétien deserves to hear the truth from me keeps me going. "It was very selfish of me. I don't expect you to forgive me. I wouldn't forgive me, that's for darned sure. I mean, unless being Catholic means you *do* have to forgive me. So, yeah. Whatever on that score. The important thing is it was my choice and it was very selfish and I'm really sorry."

Chrétien is silent. I have no hint as to what he is feeling right now. His face gives nothing away. He stares at the sky. It is a warm evening, for February, and you can see clouds to the west that are lit up like they're on fire. Really angry fire. Which, is just ... appropriate. Chrétien's extended silence can only mean he's really, really angry.

We sit there without talking, and I'm just about to say goodbye, when Chrétien clears his throat like he has something to say after all.

"You have my forgiveness," he says. Just like that. Like it's no big deal. I guess we really are farther apart than I thought we were, if he doesn't even want to talk to me about what I've done.

Or about anything.

Chrétien says nothing more. He just stares at the hot spring, at the eerie mist rising off of it.

I shift, ready to stand up and walk back to town.

But just before I rise, Chrétien says he has a story to tell me.

Chapter Thirty-Two

COMING VISIBLE

Once upon a time, a poor but lovely maiden bore unto the king a beautiful daughter. Though the king was fond of the maiden, and later of the child, he, being noble, could no more marry the maiden than he could marry a boar. For kings, you know, must concern themselves with those things which will benefit the nation and not please their own fancy.

The king, in his care of the maiden, gave her to be married to a young courtier, who, though he knew little of love and less of being father to a child, nonetheless made it his labor to love them both. And in time he grew to love them deeply.

When the child had nearly reached two years of age, pestilence ran through the court of the king, and the courtier's lady and child both fell gravely ill. The pestilence passed by the courtier, as sometimes happens, and though he would have willingly yielded his life in exchange for theirs, such an

263

opportunity was not given him.

The king's mother contracted also the illness. But she took every day a decoction prepared by a famous doctor of physick, and she returned to full health, although the doctor warned her she must drink her remedy for a month and a day after health had returned.

Now the king's mother was very fond of her bastard granddaughter. And when she learned that the child was grown ill with the pestilence, the queen visited the sick mother and child, bringing with her the physician and his remedy. The queen drank of the decoction and, despite its price being more than a wealthy man's land might yield in ten years of plenty, she shared some of it with the child and both her parents, "lest the father should grow ill as well."

The child's father remained, as ever, in good health, but the queen's remedy had come too late to return the mother and child to health. Their decline continued and in time, they left this world for the next, leaving the courtier behind. His grief was very great, and at times he thought it would be better to end his own life than to continue with his grief.

Now the courtier's father was a wise baron who had, through an unusual gift, extended his own life to many times that which is usually given to men. And in all this time, the baron had loved and lost several who had been dear to him. He did not, now, wish to lose his only son as well as having lost his daughter-in-law and his adopted grandchild. So he explained to his son that time was a great healer of grief and proposed that his son sleep for a century in an enchanted slumber such as the sleeping beauty of the wood had done once upon a time.

The courtier, loving his father greatly, agreed to enter the *enchanted slumber.*

A century passed, and the baron returned asking, "My son, are you now healed enough to return to the land of the visible?"

But after the first and the second and the third century, the courtier's answer was always the same. "Father, my grief is too great for me. I will remain apart from the visible world for yet a longer time in the hopes that one day I may rejoin you."

One day, the baron learned that a descendant of his beloved sweetheart, long dead, lived under the threat of an evil lord. And the baron, who had to devote himself to battling the evil lord, was in great distress as to how he might on the one hand battle his enemy and on the other hand protect the descendant of his beloved. So, the baron asked of his son a great favor.

"My son, will you undertake to protect this young woman, who is sought at all times by the evil lord, for I live in great fear he will utterly destroy her and all her family."

The son agreed, for he knew what it was to lose someone precious to death, and he wished to save his father from the like grief. The son feared that his days would be still heavy with sorrow, but he found, as he became accustomed once more to living in the land of the visible, that his heart was able to hold a measure of joy alongside his constant sorrow.

Of all the things he had abandoned during his enchanted slumber, laughter and a merry heart were what he had counted as his greatest losses. And the courtier, transported to a new land with neither a court nor a king, found much joy in passing his days in companionship with a raven-haired maiden whose heart was given at all times to merriment. And with each passing day, the heart of the former courtier grew by tiny increases toward wholeness.

One day, the same evil lord who had threatened the descendant of the baron's sweetheart stole away the raven-haired maiden. The courtier was in great distress to save the maiden from the evil lord. But when the courtier went to challenge the evil lord, the courtier was struck down by a powerful weapon. Although he was not killed, the courtier's wound was grave, and he was no longer in a fit state to rescue the raven-haired maiden.

His despair at this time was great, but friends of the courtier came to the castle and succeeded where he had failed, utterly defeating the evil lord and his henchmen.

At this time, the courtier's heart warmed even more greatly toward the maiden who had supplied so much mirth. But the courtier feared that to give his heart a second time would be a kind of disloyalty to his first wife.

Shortly after the defeat of the evil lord, the courtier found himself one day perusing the diary kept by his wife, wherein she charged him, should she perish, to fear not to love again. "And see that you look with your heart," she wrote, "for it sees what the eye sometimes cannot."

Now, the courtier was very troubled at this, and uncertain whether his wife's advice was good or ill-judged. For, though the courtier felt a new love warming his heart, he felt also the pull of the old love. Moreover, he feared to offer his love which came from a trammeled and not an undamaged heart.

He yearned to walk free in matters of love even as he walked free from his enchanted slumber. And he yearned for the raven-haired maiden whose heart was merry and true like that of the Cendrillon. But he was held as though with a magical bond by two items which tied him still to the past—a book and *a slipper.*

And then, as if in a fairytale, he found himself one day bereft of one of the first item that bound him, and though he expected this would cause him great pain, he found instead that the loss of the book provided him with a measure of freedom. And then, after the passage of several days, the second item that bound him was lost to him as well. Once again, where he expected great pain, he found instead a new measure of freedom.

Now, at this time, another battle with the son of the evil lord ensued, and the courtier's thoughts were occupied once more with the arts of war and with the protection of the raven-haired maiden, whom he greatly feared to lose. And when finally the evil lord was thwarted, the courtier took a day to consider all that had befallen him.

He thought of his losses, and the centuries spent in enchanted slumber. He thought of his return to the visible world, and the delight afforded him by the company of the raven-haired maiden. And he saw that by living so much in the past, he had allowed his grief to consume him.

With the magical bonds broken, the courtier discovered he was finally free. His wife and daughter would live on in his memory, but their memory would no longer consume him. And as he pondered deeply all that had befallen him, he was able to see that there was more to his transformation than the loss of the book and the shoe.

For Love had begun as well to work within him. And he saw that he desired nevermore to be parted from the raven-haired maiden, who, though she was sometimes wild and all times a source of confusion, was nonetheless all his heart's joy and all its desire.

Chapter Thirty-Three

SO LIKE THE WINGS OF RAVENS

When I look up, I see tears tracing their way down Chrétien's face.

It's one of those moments where you can feel The Kiss coming. And believe me when I say I have some familiarity with The Moment before The Kiss. But I don't want this to be just another one in my long string of Moments.

Fortunately, Chrétien doesn't seem quite as clued in regarding Moments. He is making no move to bring our lips together. In fact, he's preoccupied examining his hands right now.

"You came to me with an apology upon your lips," he says. "I hope you can see that none was necessary."

Oh, it was necessary, I'm about to say, but

Chrétien keeps talking.

"I hope you will forgive me for speaking so boldly, howsoever I cloaked it in the guise of a story," says Chrétien.

"But I love your stories," I say.

After that, we sit quietly for a minute. Staring at the spring. Staring at the evening stars popping out. Staring at anything but one another.

"So," I say, "can we maybe back it up to the part where you said you didn't want to lose me?" My voice is soft and I can't quite meet his eyes. "How *much*, exactly, do you, um, not want to lose me?"

"*Mademoiselle*," he says in this quiet voice that makes actual shivers run down my arms. "I would never be parted from your hair so like the wings of ravens. I would be always within sight of these eyes, slanted to an angle the most perfect for ensnaring the hearts of men."

"Oh." It's all I can say. All the other words I used to know, whether English or French or Chinese, have rippled clean out of my brain. "Oh."

Chrétien sighs and looks at me like I'm the anti-serum that will save his bacon. This is an actual facial expression, and I am the one who discovers it.

And now, we sort of fall into one another, hands and arms and waists and lovely, oh-so-lovely mouths. And this is when I discover it is one thing to kiss a boy you like, but it is quite another thing to kiss a man you love.

As our lips brush and pull apart, I manage to ask a

269

question. "The story you told me—did you get all the way to the end this time?"

Chrétien pulls back and looks at me with such piercing earnestness that I flush and drop my eyes. When he speaks, it is in a low voice, husky with emotion. "I am very much in hopes, *Mademoiselle*, that I have only reached the beginning of the story."

THE END

For information on all releases by Cidney Swanson:
cidneyswanson.com

Acknowledgements

"Tell the story you want to read," we are told again and again as writers. Well, as you might have guessed, the tale of Cinderella has always been one of my favorites. Re-imagining it as something Charles Perrault might have observed at the French court in his youth was enormously fun, and I hope diehard fans of his fairytale won't be too put off by my version. In fact, I hope you are inspired to have your own *Cinderella*-palooza with the peeps you treasure. I recommend combining the event with chocolate over either popcorn or pâté, however.

For this tale, focused as it was on Gwyn Li, I owe special thanks to Isabel for the concept of "Gwynitude." However, it is Katie who gets an even more basic thank you. Katie, I am so glad you kept asking me, "What is Gwyn's last name?" until I finally, *finally* found the answer all those years ago. Getting to know Gwyn's family story has been oh, so much fun, and I couldn't have done that without your seemingly innocuous question.

To my dear readers and all those friends who encourage me to write harder, write more, and write better: my sincerest gratitude. You make it all worthwhile!

0574

Made in the USA
Columbia, SC
02 August 2017